# THE EAGLE

## Clan Ross of the Hebrides

Pink Door Publishing


Print Edition



ISBN: 978-1-939356-92-5

## Also By Hildie McQueen

Clan Ross of the Hebrides

The Lion: Darach

The Beast: Duncan

The Eagle: Stuart

The Fox: Caelan

The Stag: Artair

The Hunter: Ella

Clan Ross Series

A Heartless Laird

A Hardened Warrior

A Hellish Highlander

A Flawed Scotsman

A Fearless Rebel

A Fierce Archer

Moriag Series

Beauty and the Highlander

The Lass and the Laird

Lady and the Scot

The Laird's Daughter

# Clan Ross of the Hebrides

This fictional story takes place at the beginning of the 17th century in the Scottish Hebrides, isles off the Isle of Skye's western coasts.

In the 1500s, lordship over the Hebrides collapsed and the power was given to clan chiefs. The MacNeil, in Barra, The Macdonald (Clanranald), in South Uist, The Uisdein, in North Uist and the MacLeod, the isles of Harris and Lewis.

For this series, I have moved the clans around a bit to help the story work better. The clans' locations in my books are as follows. The MacNeil will remain in Barra, The Macdonald (Clanranald) is moved to North Uist, The Uisdein resides in Benbecula, and the MacLeod remains in the Isles of Harris and Lewis. My fictional clan, Clan Ross, will laird over South Uist.

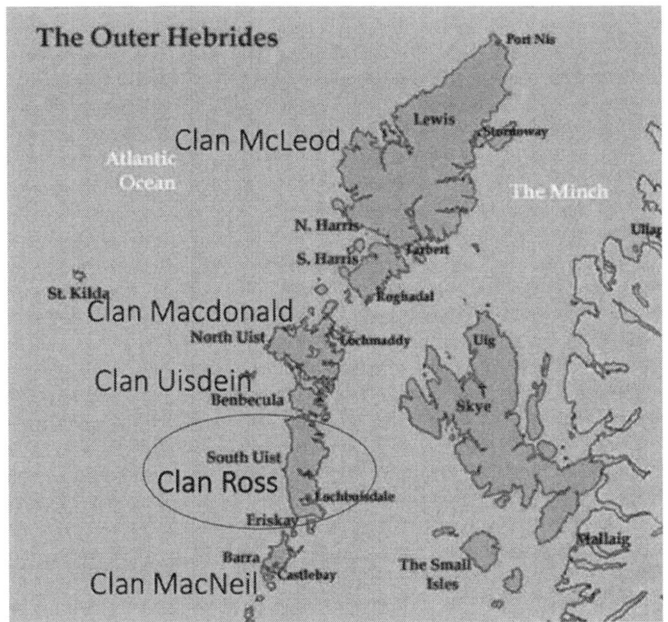


*Clan Ross of the Hebrides Map*

After the death of their father, Laird Calum Ross, the Ross siblings learn of the atrocities he committed against the clan. They must work hard to regain the people's trust and begin anew.

Each of the seven Ross siblings come to terms with their new roles as leaders responsible for hundreds of families.

One by one, they will find their calling, their place, and hopefully a love for all time.

# PROLOGUE

*South Uist, Hebrides, Scotland*
*1802*

ONE OF STUART Ross' duties as guard was to patrol the house where the refugee men lived. The house was located between the Ross keep and the house where his brothers, Duncan and Caelan, lived. He always looked forward to the trip because it meant time alone with his thoughts, and he could return in time for last meal.

His warhorse trotted sideways, its huge hooves lifting and lowering from the ground in dainty steps.

"Stop it," Stuart said to the horse who paid him no heed and added a head bob to its repertoire. Annoyed at the animal's antics Stuart gritted his teeth and pulled back on the reins. The horse seemed to be in some sort of mood continuing its odd walk.

"What is wrong with ye? Warhorses do not prance," Stuart barked.

A chuckle came from somewhere between the trees. Whoever it was must have overheard him.

"Who's there?" Stuart asked while looking into the foliage.

"It is I, Mister Stuart." A willowy young woman appeared. She wore the distinct faded clothing of someone of little means. A drab, but very clean dress, over it a tidy apron. Her hair was covered with a kerchief, pulling it back from her pretty face.

"I apologize. I overheard ye scolding yer horse," she said, lifting her gaze. Her eyes were a light brown, framed with long thick lashes.

She was the new kitchen maid who'd recently began working at the keep.

"Cait, what are ye doing so far from the keep?"

"I live just past there." She pointed behind her.

It seemed rather far from the keep, but he didn't comment. Instead, he looked to see what she held.

The young woman blinked and swallowed nervously. "I snared a rabbit to share with my mother and younger brother for super," she said, holding up a dead hare. "I have the laird's permission. I assure ye," she quickly added.

Untying his bow from the saddle, he pulled an arrow from the quiver. Cait paled, her eyes not leaving his face.

Pulling back, he released the arrow into nearby bushes. "Now ye have two."

"Th-thank ye," she stuttered turning to where he'd shot.

Stuart nodded. "Be with care, Cait."

He urged his horse forward but couldn't help looking over his shoulder to see what the woman did.

Cait remained rooted to the spot hand lifted in farewell.

Interesting that he'd not noticed how beautiful she was—before now.

# CHAPTER ONE

STUART ROSS SAT atop his horse on a ridge above the shore, along with twenty other archers, bows at the ready. Below them, atop their own huge warhorses was his brother, Laird Darach Ross, flanked by his other brothers, Duncan, and Gideon. They were in turn surrounded and well protected by skilled warriors.

Everyone was tense and ready for whatever would happen next, as just offshore a line of bìrlinns had arrived. Their banners high on the masts declaring them to be Clan Maclean.

It was not a totally unexpected visit, but it was an unwelcome one. The Maclean had not bothered to send a messenger ahead to announce the upcoming visit. Instead, the man had shown up without warning and only that morning had sent someone to proclaim his arrival. His ploy showed not only a lack of tact, but also why he was not well-liked by other lairds.

Ross and Maclean clans were not on good terms, but neither were they enemies. The animosity between them had endured from when they'd warred decades earlier.

This current visit probably had to do with Clan Ross taking in a group of men seeking asylum in early winter. Their leader, a man by the name of Lennox, claimed he and the other men had left Clan Maclean fearing execution.

Apparently, their defection was not taken lightly; because

instead of sending an emissary, Laird Maclean traveled to see about the issue personally.

Even from a distance, it was easy for Stuart to tell who The Maclean was as he rode toward Darach. An older man with gray hair shinning in the sunlight was one of the few who'd brought a horse. He was slight and looked almost childlike compared to Darach, who was younger, taller, and well built.

At times like these, Stuart was not fond of his role as archer because it meant remaining in the background. An archer's position was behind the warrior lines, which meant being far from the conversations and many times also a distance from the actual battlefield.

Not that he expected there to be any sort of fight. The Maclean had only brought a small contingent of men with him ashore. And only those warriors flanking him were on horseback.

"THIS IS AN interesting turn of events," his brother Ewan, also an archer, said. "The asylum seekers have not caused any trouble since arriving. Why does the laird himself come to retrieve them?"

Stuart shrugged. "Obviously, there had to be a strong reason for the men to leave. Lennox has been reluctant to give any explanation, other than the laird believed them to be disloyal."

The Maclean's arrival meant that Lennox would have no choice. He would have to give Darach a good reason to allow him and his men to remain.

As a signal, Darach lifted his right hand and flicked his cupped hand toward the keep. It meant that he'd invited Laird Maclean to visit. As the two lairds led the way, the warriors and then he and the archers followed.

"I really am not in the mood to hear whatever this is all about," Ewan said. "I must go home and see about Catriona." His brother's wife had recently given birth to their second child—a healthy boy they'd named, Gawin—and since then, Ewan was rarely away from his family.

Stuart did not blame him. It was good to see his brother so happy and settled. With a shrug, he replied, "No reason for ye to remain. I doubt our presence is required. Go home, I will let ye know if anything of interest happens."

It would take roughly an hour to arrive back at the keep. Stuart replaced his bow, strapping it to the side of his saddle and rolled his shoulders. He'd not slept well the night before, accosted by restlessness. Being less rested made him extra alert. He never wished to be the cause of others coming to harm.

Just then a rider neared. It was his cousin, Artair Ross, whose primary duty was as a scout. "The laird requests that ye go speak to Lennox. Tell him what has happened and ask that he come to the keep." His cousin looked past him for a moment before continuing, "When ye and Lennox arrive at the keep enter through the side gate, so not to be seen by the Maclean warriors."

Stuart hated missing the discussions that would occur once the laird's arrived at the keep. "Did the Maclean state what he wants?"

Artair shook his head. "They only spoke greetings and talked about the late laird, yer father. Then the Maclean asked if he could speak to Darach in private regarding who he called 'the traitor'."

Stuart blew out a breath. “I best hurry if I am to retrieve Lennox and be back in time to help if needed.” He motioned to two warriors. “Come with me.”

“I think I will come as well,” Artair said.

THE ABANDONED BUILDING where the asylum seekers were housed had been transformed during the winter. True to his word, Lennox and his men had made extensive repairs to the walls and roof restoring the house to its former state. There was even a garden on one side that a man was tilling when they rode up.

The night they’d first discovered strangers on the shore, twenty men had set up a meager camp. Once settled into the current building, nine made the choice to leave before the weather turned any colder and had traveled south to seek a home with another clan. The eleven that remained seemed content with their new living arrangements.

Upon Stuart and the warriors nearing the house, Lennox came out, his gaze wary.

“Has the Maclean arrived then?” he asked.

“Aye,” Stuart said dismounting along with Artair. “He and my brother are at the keep now.”

“Is he demanding we be turned over to him?” the man who’d been tilling asked, as he walked over and joined Lennox. Another pair of men came from the house and listened with interest as well.

When Stuart hesitated, Lennox motioned to the door. “Should we discuss this inside?”

He and Artair walked inside what had been a dilapidated structure. Stuart was impressed with all the work they had done. The interior had been transformed into a beautiful home.

Support beams had been replaced, and furniture built. A long table with benches filled half of the large room. There were a pair of chairs by the large hearth, and cots lined two opposite walls. Five on one side, six on the other.

The men gathered and Stuart motioned to the table. Understanding their worry, he had to tell them something, but there wasn't really any information to impart.

"Laird Maclean, along with a small contingent came to shore today. He and my brother are to have a private conversation upon their arrival at the keep."

The men murmured among themselves, several looking toward the cots, probably mentally deciding what to take. They had not come this far only to give up.

"We can leave." The statement from Lennox was soft, but resolute.

"Nay. My brother wishes to speak to ye. He asked that ye come to the keep with me. We are to enter through a secret entrance so ye are not seen by the Maclean men."

"How do we know ye will not take us captive and turn us over to the Maclean?" one of the men asked.

"If we wished to imprison ye, we would have done so by now," Artair snapped. "Ye should have expected that sooner or later, Clan Maclean would come in search of ye."

Lennox looked to the men who seemed to consider him their leader. "Laird Ross has been a kind host and I trust him. I will go and see what the Maclean wants. Remain here. I will send word."

"I can assure ye that my brother is not inclined to turn ye

away," Stuart informed the men. "Ye have posed no threat to our clan and we hold ye in high esteem."

The men seemed to take in what he said, but still exchanged looks as if considering whether to flee or remain. Stuart did not blame them.

As they rode toward the keep, Lennox gave Stuart a curious look. "Who came with the Maclean?"

"Just the small contingent of warriors. There are four bìrlinns. Two men remained with each one."

Lennox frowned. "Ye were with yer brother? Ye know what was said?"

"Nay, I was on the ridge a distance away. I could not hear anything." He did not mention that Artair had heard the conversation.

"But yet ye could see everything so clearly?"

Stuart shrugged. "I have very good eyesight."

They rode a bit longer before Lennox spoke.

"Ye and the laird look nothing alike." Lennox seemed eager to make conversation. It was probable he was nervous about what awaited.

"Darach is son to my father's first wife. The rest of us are sons to his second wife, except for Caelan, who is bastard born."

"I see," Lennox said. "Yer brother Caelan comes often and gives us work."

"Aye, I am aware," Stuart said. "He has a lot of land to maintain around his house. I am glad that ye and yer men have been able to earn a living."

The warrior was quiet for a few minutes. "Five of my men wish to work as Laird Ross' guards. Do ye think it will be possible?"

Stuart understood the need to find work doing what one knew best. He would always prefer to be an archer over anything else. "Let us see how this visit goes and then we can speak to my brother."

The man nodded and let out a sigh. "I do not understand why the Maclean would wish for us to return. There is nothing to be gained from men who are not loyal to the one in charge."

"It could be a matter of pride?"

Lennox nodded. "Aye, perhaps."

UPON ARRIVING AT the keep and stowing Lennox in a room near the maid's quarters, Stuart went to seek out his eldest brother.

Darach and the Maclean were in the great room. It seemed the hospitality portion of the visit continued.

When Stuart walked closer, Darach motioned to him. "This is Stuart, third-born son."

The Maclean looked to him with disinterest, but he managed a nod and a slight lift to the corners of his lips. If Stuart was to guess between a smile and a sneer, he would guess the latter.

Upon closer inspection, he saw the man's gray hair was actually quite thin. It was more likely his scalp Stuart had seen shining in the sunlight earlier, as it was showing between the limp strands of remaining hair that for whatever reason the man chose to wear long, hanging well past his chin. There was also a yellowing to the Maclean's skin that told of failing health. At the same time, by the narrowed eyes and pinched brow, he fought to not show the pain he was in.

Stuart recognized the gleam in the Maclean's eyes. He should, he'd seen it often enough in his late father's gaze. It could be that the man was not there so much for the men who he called traitors, but to see what he could gain as recompense for what he considered an insult.

When he met Darach's gaze, it was obvious his brother saw it as well.

The Maclean had not brought his wife, nor did any other women accompany him. Therefore, Isobel, Darach's wife, and the other women of the keep were not present. Instead, the long tables in the great room were filled with the warriors who'd come with the laird. The men ate and drank, speaking in low tones. From their wariness, the Maclean must have warned them to be on guard, or something of the like.

To ensure the family was well protected, Darach had stationed his guardsmen—double the number the Maclean had brought—throughout the hall. Some sat at tables, separate from the other clan, with their own tankards and platters of bread and cheese to share, while other warriors were on duty guarding the entrance. Further assurance was provided by Darach's personal attendants, who stood at his back.

Stuart reluctantly went to the high board and sat next to a man who'd accompanied the Maclean. The man looked to be close to his own age of two and thirty. Unlike the Maclean, this man had the bored look of someone who wished to be anywhere but there.

"I am Liam Maclean, second-born son," the man said in greeting. "My father introduced me to yer other brothers before ye entered."

The man then looked toward the entrance from which Stuart had come, seeming to calculate why he'd arrived so much later.

He blew out a breath. "How far is the local village?"

"A bit over an hour's ride."

A young maid appeared with a large tray. She walked to the head table, gaze downcast and placed a tankard in front of him.

Stuart realized who it was. "Cait, did ye and yer mother make a good rabbit stew?"

Cait's gaze lifted, and her lips curved. "Aye, Mister Stuart. She asked that I thank ye for the second rabbit."

"Is a rabbit all it takes to spend time with ye?" Liam asked while leering at Cait, who's eyes widened and cheeks turned a crimson red.

She hastily placed the food down before them and dashed away.

"That comment was unacceptable," Stuart spoke in a low menacing tone. "Ye will not disrespect the women while in my home."

"'Tis but a mere maid," Liam said with an eye roll. "No one of importance."

"I will not repeat myself." Stuart took a long draw from his tankard, to keep from saying or doing something he'd regret.

Across the room, Cait's half brother, Torac, watched with interest. The warrior's gaze moved from the high board to his sister.

Just then Darach spoke to the laird in a louder tone, so that everyone could hear. "I insist that ye and yer men remain for the night. It will soon be too late to return across the sea to yer home."

"I accept on behalf of myself, my son, and my men," the Maclean replied. "As a matter of fact, I beg of yer hospitality for two or three more days. I have many things to discuss with ye."

Blank of expression, Darach nodded his agreement.

It was much later that the lairds adjourned to Darach's study. Stuart, Liam, and Duncan were asked to join them. Gideon, the youngest, as well as Artair would remain in the great hall to ensure order between their guards and the Maclean's, who seemed to take an instant dislike of each other.

Once in the study, the men were poured whiskey and they settled into comfortable chairs.

The Maclean inventoried the room, not bothering to hide his curiosity. "I met yer father only the one time he came to visit me. I never felt the need to cross the water to come here. I find sea travel most discomfiting."

Despite the fact he'd not been aware their father had ever visited a man so disliked by all the surrounding lairds, Darach managed to hide his surprise.

"Not everyone is fond of water travel," Darach said with an accommodating tone. "We venture out a great deal by bìrlinn. I do not mind it."

"Let us get to the reason for my visit," Laird Maclean said suddenly. A tactic to throw off whoever he spoke to, by abruptly changing the subject. "All of the traitors must be returned to me immediately to be punished. I will accept nothing less."

Darach sipped his whiskey slowly with his gaze averted

and remained silent. A trait that often discomfited whomever he opposed. It was humorous when the Maclean and Liam exchanged confused looks as the long stretch of silence continued.

Use to Darach's processing of information, Stuart downed his drink and rose to pour another. "I do believe the weather should be favorable to traveling for the next few days," he said to the Maclean. "However, I agree with ye. I too prefer to travel by land rather than water."

The Maclean didn't reply. Instead, he looked at Darach, who looked to Stuart, glass still in hand.

"What…" the Maclean began, but stopped talking when Darach gave him a pointed look.

His brother let out a breath. "No."

Once again, the Maclean and Liam exchanged puzzled looks.

It was Liam who spoke next. "What do ye mean no? It is not a request Laird Ross. My father has rights over those men."

"Does he?" Darach asked with a flat tone. One that Stuart knew meant his brother thoroughly disliked the men he spoke to.

Darach looked to Stuart. "What do we know about the men?"

"They came asking for asylum from ye. Stated that they had fled for their lives. We know nothing more. Winter meant they were contained to a certain place and most of them have stayed there since."

"Most?" Liam asked, his expression incredulous.

"Half of the men have since left."

The Maclean's eyes rounded. "Ye allowed half of them to

escape?"

"They are not our prisoners," Stuart replied. "They may come and go as they please."

Liam jumped to his feet. "Those men are traitors to my father; they must face the consequences of their disobedience."

Suddenly the Maclean's countenance changed, and he gave them an appeasing look. "Be calm son. Let us not start off by arguing."

"What other subject do ye propose we speak of then?" Darach asked.

"I would like to get to know ye better," the Maclean said, meeting Darach's gaze. "As a new laird, I am sure ye have much to learn. Perhaps I can provide guidance while here. For now, I will not press the issue of the men, ye hold."

Every word the man uttered grated. Stuart met Darach's eyes and understood his brother was on the brink of losing control.

"Why don't we proceed to the courtyard. I will show ye the new guard training areas," Stuart said motioning to the door.

As he walked out with the Maclean's, he noted that Duncan moved closer to a very furious Laird Ross.

# CHAPTER TWO

CAIT'S HEART POUNDED so hard, she thought it would burst out of her chest. She leaned on a wall just outside the kitchen, tears threatening to spill down her cheeks.

"Whatever is the matter with ye child?" Greer, the cook, asked giving her a questioning look. "There is much to do for ye to give into fret."

"I'm sorry," Cait replied lifting her apron to wipe her face. "It's just that one of the men visiting said something upsetting, that is all."

Greer shook her head and motioned for Cait to follow her. "Men are horrible creatures at times." The cook hurried to where her daughter ladled out hot figs mixed with honey into pastry shells. "Do not be so sloppy, Finella."

Cait lifted two pitchers and prepared to go back out. She said a silent prayer no one would bother her. But each time there were visitors, someone always seemed to take notice of her and do or say something untoward.

The men who worked at the keep knew her half brother, Torac, a warrior for the laird. Not wishing a confrontation with the muscled warrior, meant most of the Ross men let her be. However, visitors were another story.

As she refilled the tankards of the Maclean men at the long tables, several pretended to stretch or lift their hands, touching her arm or backside. Cait was adept at avoiding most of them, over time maids became prolific at sensing where to stand and how to turn to stay out of reach.

When she walked past where her brother stood, Torac took her by the arm. "Ye should do yer best to remain in the kitchen. Ask Greer to give ye other tasks."

"I cannot," Cait replied. "I have only been working here a few weeks. I do not want to be any trouble."

He glared in the direction of the visitors and nodded understanding. Cait went about her duties feeling better at knowing her half brother watched over her.

Just six weeks earlier, she, her mother, and her young brother had traveled from the southern portion of the isle to seek help from Torac. Her mother was ill and Cait needed work in order to support them.

Her father had been married to Torac's mother. It wasn't until he'd not returned for a long time that they'd discovered the truth from a traveling peddler. Not only about a second family, but that her father had died.

Thankfully Torac had been kind enough to petition the laird for work for Cait. The laird had also been overly generous and allowed them to move into an empty cottage on the lands. The walk back and forth from the keep was quite long, but most days Cait didn't mind it. As tired as she was at the end of the day, she looked forward to returning home rather than sleeping in the maid's quarters.

Before arriving at Ross lands, her mother had spent most days inside, and her younger brother—who was four and ten—did his best to look after her. For months her mother had languished in bed, seeming to have no will to continue in day-to-day life. However, since they'd arrived there six weeks ago, her mother seemed to regain a bit of strength every day.

Cait's was not an easy life, but neither was it horrible.

After the meal and cleaning of the great hall, Cait joined the line of servants awaiting Greer's instructions. She stood between Finella and another new kitchen maid, Cora. In the short time they'd worked together, the three of them had become good friends.

"With so many to feed and see after, we will have a lot of work for the next few days," Greer informed them.

The woman's bright eyes told that she didn't mind one bit.

"Ye love it when we have visitors," Finella said with a roll of her eyes. "I do not understand ye mum."

"It is our calling to see after the laird's family and their visitors. Why should we not be glad?" Greer replied and then spoke to Cait. "Unfortunately, ye will have to remain here tonight and possibly tomorrow as well."

Cait's mind immediately went to home. There wasn't any way she could send word. Her mother would fret, but she also knew at times Cait had to work long hours. Hopefully, she wouldn't worry overmuch.

Greer continued, "The visiting Maclean men will be housed with our guards, which means ye should be able to stay away from them."

When duties were given, Cait and Cora were assigned the great hall. Her heart sank at realizing she'd have to face the dreadful man who'd come with the Maclean, again.

"I prefer serving," Cora said and held up a bandaged arm. "Burns hurt."

Once the meal and preparation assignments were given,

Cait hurried outside to the garden to fetch turnips that would accompany the roasted lamb.

Just as she walked out, she noted that a man paced beside the garden gate. It was Stuart Ross and he seemed to be deep in thought. Cait tried to figure out how she could get around him and into the garden without bothering him.

As if sensing her, he looked up.

"I must go into the garden," she said pointing to the gate.

He frowned for a moment, as if not quite understanding. Then upon noting he blocked her progress, opened the gate, and motioned for Cait to enter.

To her shock, he followed. "I spoke to Liam Maclean and made it clear we do not tolerate that kind of behavior. He will not bother ye again."

Her breath stopped and she could barely swallow. "Ye spoke to him for me? Ye should not have bothered. It is most… kind. Thank ye, Mister Stuart."

When his lips curved, she couldn't look away. Stuart Ross was incredibly handsome, with shoulder-length dark wavy hair, long lashes, and the familiar Ross hazel eyes.

"Ye do not have to thank me." He looked to the garden. "What are ye going to serve me to eat?"

The question was asked as if she were to cook for him. The intimate way he phrased it made her face heat immediately. "Turnips. Greer is making roasted lamb with turnips."

He made a face. "I do not care for turnips. But do not dare tell Greer." He walked out of the garden, carefully closing the small gate behind him.

Cait stood rooted to the spot her gaze glued to his retreating back.

The interaction had been quite strange. Had he been waiting to speak to her? Why would a man of his standing take time to come and inform her of a conversation he'd had with someone of the same? Although she was new to life in the keep, Cait knew enough to realize this was most unusual.

She looked to the window and met Greer's gaze and for a moment Cait froze, unsure what to do. It was hard to decipher Greer's look. Hopefully, it didn't mean she'd be scolded for conversing with the laird's brother.

This was most troubling. All she wanted to do was work, earn a wage, and take care of her family. It would be best to try to avoid any contact with men at the keep from now on, other than her brother.

Deep in thought, she lowered to her knees and dug up the turnips along with one large potato.

When she entered the kitchen with the items in her apron, Greer motioned to the table and tapped Finella's shoulder. "Be a dear, peel and cut them into evenly sized pieces."

Greer's alert gaze met Cait's. "Was there a problem with Mister Stuart?"

Cait shook her head. "He asked if he could have something other than turnips."

Greer chuckled. "He thinks I do not know he dislikes them. I had hoped he would learn to."

Relieved when Greer did not ask anything more, Cait hurried about her tasks managing to avoid most of the people in the keep until finished.

At least meal, she and Cora served those in the great room. Along with the guests, there were only a few others present. And though it was none of her concern—since what happened between the lairds had little to do with the servants—the air in the room was subdued.

She did her best to keep her distance from the men at the high board, which worked well. Keeping her gaze downcast also helped to keep from seeing the unlikable visitor and avoiding Stuart Ross as well.

When she went to the table where the ladies of the household sat, the laird's wife, Isobel, touched Cait's lower arm. "Are ye unwell? Ye seem nervous."

Cait adored the laird's wife. Since arriving, Isobel had always made her feel welcome and often asked about her mother and brother. "I am well Lady Ross. Thank ye for asking."

The laird's mother, Lady Mariel, gave her a quizzical look. "Where do ye live Cait?"

Knowing she'd be in trouble for lingering while Cora had to continue serving, Cait let out a soft sigh. "In a cottage that yer son, my laird, was gracious enough to allow my mother, younger brother, and me to live in. It is near a creek. We are very grateful for it."

"I am glad to know." Seeming to understand she had to continue with her duties, the woman smiled and returned her attention to the other women at the table.

Cait hurried back to the kitchen where Greer immediately handed her a tray laden with sweet cakes.

The meal lasted longer than usual. It seemed the visiting laird and his son enjoyed late evenings and partaking of what was offered. Her feet ached as once again she refilled the empty cups of the men who lingered. Most of the room was empty except for the Maclean, his son, Darach, Stuart, and Duncan. The few others that remained were the usual sentries and the laird's personal guards.

Not wishing to look at the visiting laird's son, Cait kept her gaze downcast, though she could feel his gaze on her. Once when she'd dare to look from under her lashes, her suspicions were confirmed, he was tracking her every move.

"The potato was delicious," Stuart said, startling her so that the liquid she poured sloshed over the edge of his cup and onto the tabletop.

"I-I . . ." She grabbed a cloth from a pocket on her apron to clean the spill. "I am glad." Cait dared to look up for a scant second to meet his gaze and instantly her face heated at his regard.

"Ye scared the poor lass." She heard his brother, Duncan, say to Stuart as she moved away.

In the kitchen, Greer sat at the table fanning her face with a cloth but had a bright smile at seeing Cait's empty tray.

"Ye can tell a great deal about a person by the way they treat their hosts," the cook said shaking her head.

"What do ye mean?" Cait asked, lowering to a chair across from the woman.

"If they have little concern for their guest's nightly routines and need for rest, then they are not kind people."

Cait drank lukewarm cider and hungrily gobbled some leftover bread upon which she placed a thin slice of cold meat. "I agree," she replied between bites.

Cora entered looking entirely limp, her face drawn with exhaustion. "I am so tired," she complained, but upon seeing the tray of leftovers that Greer had set out for them, she slumped into a chair. "They are finally going to their bed-chambers."

"We will wait a bit and then clean up. It won't be too long," Greer said attempting to make light of the hard work ahead.

"Lads," she called out to the two sleeping boys who were to help with cleaning. "Go fetch the dirty dishes."

The boys sat up yawned and stretched but didn't move. One of them, who looked to be about two and ten frowned. "Is it morning?"

Greer chuckled. "It will be soon. So go on and hurry. Get yer job done so ye can get more sleep before I wake ye for morning duties."

Moments later, Cait and Cora trudged to the great room to complete the tasks of the night. Greer was right, morning would come much too soon.

IN THE STUDY, Darach was livid. His nostrils flared as he looked to Stuart and Duncan. "An entire day of nothing but revelry and drink. The man has not yet explained what he expects now that I've said I won't turn the men over to him."

"I do not believe he has any plan, nor does he care really about the men who came seeking asylum. He is here and behaving in such a manner because he believes we owe him an apology," Stuart explained.

"I will do no such thing," Darach roared, living up to his moniker of being called: *The Lion.*

There was something else, but Stuart couldn't quite put his finger on it. Laird Maclean was old and didn't seem to have a clear reason for staying longer. However, there was a reason, and he would find out what it was.

Apparently, Duncan thought along the same lines. "Perhaps he has something very important to impart or to ask ye and is waiting for the right time"

Stuart nodded in agreement. "What if we hold an archery competition? The laird announced they would remain for an additional two days. Since we cannot spend the entire time waiting for him to tell us the true reason for the visit. Perhaps if we distract them, he or his son will talk.

"Highland hospitality," Duncan all but spit out the words. "We should send them on their way. They take advantage."

Of all the brothers, Duncan was the least diplomatic. If he had been named laird, times like these would have been quite entertaining. Then again, they would probably be at war with at least two clans by now.

"I wonder if he has any alliances on the Hebrides?" Darach said, ignoring Duncan's outburst. "If he's friends with, let's say, the Uisdein, then we may have something to worry about."

Stuart frowned. "I doubt that bastard would try anything against us after taking ye prisoner." The Uisdein had imprisoned Darach when he'd gone to ask about a man named Cairn, who'd disappeared after attempting to start an uprising against the Ross's.

"The Maclean and the Uisdein do have something in common," Darach acknowledged, scratching his chin. "Both feel slighted by us."

"We should reinforce the guards on our northern border just in case." Duncan blew out a breath. "I will go with twenty men. Beatrice will be protected as Caelan will not allow anything to happen to her."

For many years, Caelan and Duncan shared a huge house south of the keep. When Duncan married Beatrice, she along with her companion, Orla, came to live there as well.

"Very well. Go get rest and then depart in the morning."—Darach hesitated—"Wait until after first meal. Let us see if the laird deems it time to disclose something."

# CHAPTER THREE

A LIGHT ACROSS her face brought Cait out of deep slumber. She immediately sat up with a gasp. Why had she been allowed to sleep in so late? Or perhaps she'd not heard the knocks when morning call had come.

She dressed in haste and winced as she stood and began walking. Her feet remained sore from the long day before.

Upon entering the busy kitchen, she understood. She was ushered aside as women passed by heading to the great room with trays laden with food. Cait almost wept with gratefulness at seeing that Greer had sent for several women from the village to help with the kitchen work that morning.

"Once ye break yer fast, see about vegetables for last meal," Greer instructed. The older woman bustled about the kitchen giving out instructions to those cooking and others filling platters and bowls.

How the woman found so much energy, Cait was not sure.

"What do ye wish for me to harvest?" Cait asked. "There is not much yet. The plantings are young."

The woman stopped to consider. "Aye, ye are correct. We will make meat pies for last meal. Go to the village and see if ye can purchase something there. Anything will do."

Cait had hoped to go see about her mother and brother that day, but since the visiting laird had extended his visit, it would probably not be possible.

Making a list in her mind of what was left at the house for them to eat, she realized there wasn't much.

"May I take some bread to my mother and brother?" she asked doing her best to ignore the pang of embarrassment. "They may not have anything left to eat as I have not been able to bring food."

Greer continued to watch as the two maids filled bowls, then lifted the trays and walked out. "Ye have time to go home and check on them. Just be sure to be quick about it. Take the sack there." She pointed to the sack in the corner. "It has what was left of yesterday's bread. And cut some of the sausage to take as well."

The head cook turned away when a woman called to ask about whatever she was stirring over the heat, so she didn't see Cait's reddened face.

That she had to beg for food was not a good feeling; however, embarrassment was a small price to pay to ensure her family were fed.

With the sack of food for her family and coins to purchase what was needed for last meal, Cait walked out the kitchen door and past the garden, to find someone to take her to the village.

It would have been an impossible task with her sore feet to walk all the way to her home and back, and then to complete her daily duties. Thankfully, with the added task of going to the village, she could use one of the carts and do both.

Upon seeing a lad, she motioned him over. "I require a cart and a horse. Can ye find one, as well as someone to take me to my family's cottage and the village?"

"I will take ye," the young man replied with earnest. "My master requires me to fetch items from there today as well."

"Can ye be gone for so long? I must stop to see my mother," Cait asked, not wishing to get him in trouble with whoever his taskmaster was.

"I will ask Mister Stuart." The young man raced away toward the side of the keep.

Curious as to what happened, Cait followed him around the side building. Men were setting up archery targets while others set up a short fence of sorts.

Standing with arms crossed watching the goings-on was the visiting laird's son. Upon spotting her, he glared in her direction.

Cait took a step back.

At the site of Stuart Ross heading toward her with the lanky lad beside him, she blew out a breath. So much for avoiding the man.

Past him she noticed that the visiting laird's son narrowed his eyes and watched them as they made their way toward her.

Stuart pulled out a purse of coin and dug into it. "Go by the tavern and get plenty of ale for last meal." Stuart handed the coins to the lad who bobbed his head enthusiastically. "Nothing else. Not even an onion pie."

"Cait, will ye please see that Anton does not linger past his task?" He gave Anton a pat on the shoulder. "Enjoy yer pie."

She couldn't help but smile at the young man's cheeks coloring. Obviously, it was a joke between him and Stuart. "I will try my best."

His gaze hesitated on her face and after a beat, he gave her a firm nod and walked away.

"Do I have something on my face?" Cait asked Anton who gave her a knowing look.

"Nay, I think he likes ye," the lad replied. "We must make haste," he added and hurried away to fetch the cart.

Cait looked over her shoulder and noted that Stuart was watching her walk away. Hurriedly she turned away.

Despite her silly heart skipping beats at seeing him and the persistent butterflies in her belly, it was not a good thing to catch the eye of a man of status. Men like Stuart Ross considered women in her position to be easy prey. To be taken and then discarded when someone else catches their eye. She'd not been there long enough to notice if the Ross men were the kind that took many lovers.

Although she'd heard rumblings among the maids about Gideon, the youngest. Most of the time, the whispers were accompanied by giggles and a great deal of fanning their faces.

Why was she spending so much time thinking about it? Cait shook her head and walked closer to the well to wait for Anton.

Across the courtyard, guards worked diligently to set up for whatever festivity was to happen. The familiar tall figure paced from a target to a specific spot and pointed to the ground. Cait sighed and then blew out an annoyed breath. The sooner she accepted that men like Stuart Ross would only marry someone of an elevated social status, the better.

CAIT TURNED TO walk away and ran into a maid carrying two buckets of water. "Watch where ye go!" the maid cried out. But it was too late. Cait had bumped into the woman and knocked one bucket to the ground, the water spilling onto the dirt.

"Oh no," Cait said grabbing the now empty bucket. "I will refill it and bring it in."

The maid huffed and hurried off with the remaining one.

IT WAS SO much faster to travel with a horse and cart. They arrived at her humble home soon after leaving the keep.

Her brother, Brice, was outside the cottage cleaning a rabbit. His wide grin made her heart squeeze with love. Despite the circumstance, he was always in a good mood.

She climbed down from the cart. "Ye snared a hare."

"Yesterday I caught five fish. Ye missed a good meal," Brice declared with a proud grin.

Cait studied him for a moment. "I am so relieved to see that ye can provide for ye and Mother when I am away. But ye mustn't be gone too long from here during the day and leave her alone."

Brice nodded. "I make certain not to be."

"Fishing?" She gave him a look. "And just how long did it take ye to catch five fish?"

"It didn't matter. I went with him." Her mother appeared at the doorway looking amazingly refreshed. "I have felt much better these last few days."

Her mother studied her for a long moment. "I was horribly worried. But Brice reminded me that there are times ye are required to remain at the keep."

"Aye, there are visitors. So, I must remain another night or two. Ye look well Mother."

"I have been boiling the herbs that Greer sent and drinking

the liquid every day as she instructed. It has helped so very much."

Cait hugged her mother. "It makes me so very happy then."

When Anton cleared his throat, Cait turned to give him a pleading look. But he shook his head.

"I must go. I wanted to bring by this bread and sausage that Greer sent. There is a visiting laird…"

Her mother interrupted, "Ye do not have to explain. When lairds visit, the work is tripled. Go dear. We are well."

After one last hug, Cait climbed onto the wagon and they continued to the village about an hour away.

"Ye live far from the keep. Do ye walk every day?" Anton asked.

"I do," Cait said. "It is a long walk. Sometimes I am fortunate to come across someone traveling to the keep. Most days by the time I arrive, I am tired before my chores begin."

"Yer brother is old enough to be a squire. If both of ye work for the laird, ye can ask to live at the keep."

Cait shook her head. "I do not wish for my brother to become a warrior or a guard. I cannot bear to lose him in battle."

"What would ye have him do then?"

She could not think of a reply. "I suppose whatever it is he wishes to do." After a moment she asked, "What do ye do for Mister Stuart?" Cait liked Anton. He seemed pleased with his lot in life and had a pleasing demeaner.

"Everything," he said with a wide smile. "I am his squire. I do whatever he requires. He is going to train me with the bow and arrow." Anton held his left arm out and bent it at the elbow, flexing his bicep. "Always wanted to learn sword fighting. When I told Mister Stuart, he said I could never be a warrior being so slender, he suggested I consider archery."

"That is a good idea," Cait replied.

"Two of the Ross brothers are archers, Mister Ewan and Mister Stuart," Anton continued. "Both win every competition. I hate that I will miss most of it today."

"I was wondering what they were setting up for. An archery competition then?"

Anton's head bobbed. "Aye, to keep the visiting laird's son occupied. That is what Mister Stuart said."

"They may wait until later in the day to start," Cait told him. "The visiting laird seems to linger after meals."

At that Anton brightened. "We will hurry in town. Ye willna be long will ye?"

Cait shook her head. "Looking for vegetables for last meal. That is all."

It was late morning when they reached the village, so there was only a smattering of sellers in the village square. Thankfully a cheerful couple was selling peas and onions.

To the couple's delight, she purchased all they had of each. She then noted they also had collards.

"Can ye bring those to the keep? Greer will pay ye," Cait said sure Greer would agree.

"For the laird, no need for payment," the woman said with pride. "The first of the harvest." She tied several bunches of the leafy greens and handed them to her. Cait thanked them and walked toward the tavern where Anton had gone.

The young man and another older one emerged lugging large clay pots covered with rough fabric that was tied to keep the ale from spilling. Cait eyed other jugs that had been fastened to the sides of the cart. "That is a great deal of ale."

Out of breath, Anton loaded the last of the pots with the help of the older man. After they secured them to the wagon to ensure they didn't topple over, Anton finally sat down on the bench and waved to the man who hurried back inside.

"He's the owner Tom, Anton said. "He added two more since it is for the laird."

On the way back to the keep, Cait had to hold on to the bench to keep from falling at how fast Anton urged the horse to go.

"I know ye are in a hurry, but please slow down a bit. It will not do us any good if the horse breaks a leg on this uneven road. Or if the pots break."

With a sigh, Anton did as she asked.

"It is still early," she reassured him hiding a smile when he frowned.

If Cait were honest, she was also anxious to see the competition. It would be the first time she'd ever seen one at a keep. There had been games held by the villagers where she used to live, but they were usually not well organized.

"Are servants allowed to be a part and see the competition?"

Anton nodded. "Most of the time aye. Depends on yer duties."

"How long have ye squired for Mister Stuart?"

Anton grinned and frowned in concentration. "Two years soon."

Upon riding through the gates, Anton continued forth until in front of the kitchen entrance. Soon lads were summoned to help unload the ale and Cait carried her purchases into the kitchen.

"Ye must have flown to the village to have returned so soon," Greer said chuckling. "What happened? Were ye chased?"

After placing the basket down on the table, Cait smoothed her hair and blew out a breath. "Nay, Anton was in a hurry to return because of the competition. He did not wish to miss any of it."

"Ye poor dear. That boy has little sense," Greer said scowling. "He follows after Mister Stuart like a little pup."

"I must admit to being a bit scared I'd be bounced right out of the wagon," Cait added good-naturedly.

Greer peered into the basket and gave her an approving look. "Onion and lamb pies will be most delicious for last meal. The peas will be a good addition for tomorrow's meal.

Her eyes widened when a lad entered with the bundles of collards. "Where did ye find these?"

Cait explained about the couple and Greer nodded with approval. "They are good people."

The cook looked around the room. "First meal is over, there is time for a wee rest. Everyone is outside watching. Ye can sit outside the side entrance and watch if ye wish."

"Oh, thank ye." Cait hurried out of the kitchen and down the corridor past the servant's rooms to a side door that opened to a space where servants often went to rest. Cora waved her over to where she and Finella had commandeered a bench.

The west side of the courtyard had been transformed. A shelter had been set up under where seating was available for those who came to watch. Bright banners flapped in the breeze from the ropes that kept the tent in place.

At one end of the large grassy area were four large mounds that the archers often used for practice. The targets were propped on the top of the mounds and about twenty paces in front of them was a short wooden fence-like structure. This marked the boundary the archers would stand behind.

There was clapping as four men approached the short fence and stood with feet apart, bows held at the ready.

Artair Ross stood on the sideline and yelled out commands.

"Nock!"

"Mark!"

"Draw!"

"Loose!"

The commands were repeated three times. Meanwhile, those seated cheered, clapped, and exclaimed as the arrows hit the targets.

She had not lived there long enough to know the four men, so was glad when Finella told her the competitor's names.

There was a hush as someone went to inspect the targets. Apparently, it was a Maclean who'd shot best by the polite applause.

The next group was familiar. Ewan, Stuart, Gideon, and the visiting laird's son, Liam.

"Look at all the swooning," Finella muttered.

Following Finella's line of sight, Cait saw that it was true. A group of women waved handkerchiefs in the air calling out names. "Stuart! Gideon!"

"Where did the women come from?" Cait asked narrowing her eyes to see them clearer. "They are not from the keep."

"The neighboring areas. I believe an announcement was sent to let families know about the competition. Several archers came to be part of it," Finella said. "Each time Misters Stuart and Gideon are about, women gather."

Once again, Artair called out the commands. This time there were louder exclamations since the women were overly interested.

Liam Maclean made a show as he paced the distance from the fence looking where all the women were. He lifted a hand to acknowledge them, and the silly creatures whispered to each other between giggles.

"I do not care for Liam Maclean," Cora said. "Although attractive, he has the most atrocious ways."

"I agree," Finella added. "He made one of the kitchen maids cry this morning."

Cait didn't add what he'd said to her.

They withdrew the arrows from the targets, and it was time for another set of archers to compete. It seemed this time it was the best of those who'd already competed. It included Ewan, Stuart, Liam, and another Maclean archer.

Stuart stepped up to the short fence first.

Cait concentrated on watching him. His broad back flexed under the fabric of his tunic as he stretched out the bow.

When he released the arrow, there was a quiet hush.

"No one alive can beat him," Finella whispered. "Stuart Ross is the best archer in the land."

The crowd cheered when his arrow hit the target. Cait could not see how accurate his shot was, but she gathered by the applause it was good.

Liam Maclean's shot was close, but not as good as Stuart's.

And yet the silly women gathered were almost as enthusiastic when he finished.

Ewan and the other archer were next. It seemed the Ross archers were much better, but they still had to shoot one more time.

When Stuart shot again and split his own arrow, the cheers were nearly deafening. Liam's second arrow was closer to the center of the target. It was a good shot, but not as good as Stuart's. Cait had to admire that Stuart, rather than allowing the visitor to win, had instead beat him soundly.

Stuart got first place, followed by Liam, third went to Ewan, and last was the other archer.

"I believe Mister Ewan allowed Liam Maclean to beat him," Cora murmured.

"I do as well," Cait agreed.

"Time to get to work." Greer appeared at the doorway, her gaze pinning them before moving to where the archery competition took place. "Mister Stuart did exceptionally well."

"Aye," Finella said. "He did."

"Of course, he did," Greer replied. "Come along. The women are almost done with the cooking. We need to see about setting the tables."

The four of them went to the great hall. It was strange for the room to be utterly empty. Usually, there were people about before the midday meal.

Greer scanned the high board as a pair of maids walked in with brooms and began sweeping, not paying them any heed.

Lads rushed in with buckets and a younger one with large rags. "Scrub the tables well," Greer instructed.

The woman walked about the room inspecting tabletops

and chairs. "Lady Ross asked that we ensure the room is prepared for last meal. We'll do most of the work now and finish once midday meal is done."

Greer didn't leave, but instead followed behind them with a happy smile. "I have tasked the lads to roast a pig. It will be served with mashed peas. The women are baking sweet tarts. And I will cook a pudding that will not take long to complete."

As the woman spoke, Cait and Cora scrubbed the long tables and benches.

Finella worked at the round table where the Ross women sat and the table on the high board.

When Cait finished two tables and began cleaning the third, Finella hurried over and began to clean as well. Together they worked fast and before long the room was spotless, the fresh air from the open doors removing all lingering smells.

"So much better," Cait announced, standing near the front entrance. "This room stunk like rotted fish. I do not know how anyone could stand to eat in here."

"I agree," a deep voice said, and she practically jumped out of her skin.

Stuart Ross had entered. She wanted to glare at the others for not warning her. "Mister Stuart…," she began not looking to him. Unable to figure out what to say, she hurried to where the other two women were.

He scanned the room as she, Cora, and Finella stood in a line waiting to hear what he had to say.

"The competition ended." He didn't look at them, instead appearing to be considering where to sit.

"Off we go," Finella announced, and they hurriedly gathered the buckets and rags.

Greer wandered back in. “Good gracious, I do not believe to have seen the great room this clean in a long time.” She beamed at them. “Good work.”

Once again, they lined up for further instructions.

Lady Isobel and the laird’s mother, Lady Mariel entered. Both smiled widely at seeing the work that had been accomplished.

Lady Isobel looked to them. “Greer, keep the midday meal light. I believe most of the visitors will be eating outdoors.”

“I have trays prepared with bread, cheeses, and sliced cold duck my lady.”

“Delightful,” Lady Isobel said with a smile.

The women walked to the stairs to change clothing and Cait prepared to follow the others to the kitchen and empty the bucket she carried. Stuart stopped her with a touch to her arm. “Anton tells me ye have a brother who will soon be of age to squire.”

She wondered where Anton was so she could kick him in the kneecap. “I do not know what age squires should be. My brother Brice is ten and four.”

“Torac, is yer brother as well?”

That he knew so much about her made Cait nervous. “Aye. He is my half brother.”

“Torac is a good warrior. Ye should speak to him about…Brice.” The corners of his lips lifted just a bit. It was enough to make her gawk. How could a man be so handsome? “Perhaps yer brother is interested in work here at the keep.”

Swallowing past her dry throat, Cait nodded and then shook her head. “Mister Stuart if I may be frank. I am not sure what he wishes to do. He should choose his own path, do ye not agree?"

"Ye should ask him."

When the man did not move, seeming to be considering what to say next. She glanced past him to see that Lady Isobel and Lady Mariel remained at the stairs and watched them with interest.

"I should see about my duties. Thank ye for taking interest in my brother." Cait rounded him and all but ran from the great hall, doing her best not to splash dirty water from the sides of the bucket.

Hurrying past the kitchen, she exited outside to toss the dirty water out. "Hurry Cait, we need to get the trays ready," Cora called blowing out a breath. "I will be glad when the visitors leave."

"They do keep us busy."

Cait did not look over her shoulder for fear Stuart Ross had followed her.

# CHAPTER FOUR

LATER THAT DAY, Laird Maclean held court in front of the large hearth in the great hall. Surrounded by other visitors, he took delight in telling stories to anyone who would listen. The day was ending, and it seemed the visiting laird had found every excuse to not talk with Darach.

Stuart walked to where the man sat with a local family. "Laird, my brother requests yer presence."

"Aye, of course," the man replied and with a wide grin addressed the others. "Duty calls."

He walked alongside Stuart. "Are ye the only unwed brother?"

Stuart shook his head. "Gideon and Caelan are still unwed."

"I see," the man replied. "Ye are third-born, which means ye cannot aspire to much."

The man had a way of saying things that made one want to hit him. But Stuart would not be baited. "I have all I aspire for. My brother is generous."

"How so?" The laird gave him an unbelieving look. "Ye live here in the keep, I assume."

Instead of replying, he motioned to the study. "After ye." Laird Maclean made a condescending face as if to say: He knew he was right. Stuart had nothing to claim as his own.

In actuality, upon becoming laird Darach split the vast lands of Clan Ross between his brothers, giving each of them plenty of land. His lands—which were to the northwest—included a fishing village, woods with plenty of wildlife, and access to a large body of freshwater, Loch Bee. Gideon was given the lands to the north, Ewan lived on his lands just below Gideon's. Duncan and Caelan had lands to the south.

Once inside the study, the Maclean lowered to a chair next to his son. He studied Darach for a long moment.

"I demand my eldest son be returned to me immediately. Where is he? Where is Lennox?"

For a scant second Darach was taken off guard, no one would notice except for those who knew him as well as his brothers did.

It all became clear. The Maclean was dying and wished for his eldest—and next in line to be Laird Maclean—to take over his duties.

"Is it not his decision to make? Whether to return or not?" Darach asked. "I have no claim over yer son, nor can I order him to do anything."

Liam Maclean kept a blank expression. If the older brother did not return, it meant he would become laird by default. It was an interesting turn of events. Stuart understood why the younger Maclean was bitter. His father would rather travel and lower himself to admit his eldest was against him than to allow him the position.

"Lennox is headstrong. Turned against me. I would rather not go into details as to why. I wish to speak to him and then bring him and the men who are left back to Skye."

Stuart exchanged a look with Darach. "By force?"

"If need be," the Maclean barked. "He has no choice in the matter."

Darach was pensive. "Why would anyone wish for a reluctant laird?"

"It is not the lairdship he is reluctant about," Liam finally spoke. "It is returning prior to father's death."

The Maclean's head snapped toward his younger son. "Enough."

It was certainly a fascinating predicament. Given the size of the Ross army, the Maclean could not take Lennox by force. And yet, Darach could not intervene in something so personal between another laird and his son.

"Yer son is here," Darach finally said. "Whatever he and ye decide is not something I wish to be part of."

Darach motioned to Stuart. "Bring him."

"One moment," the Maclean said. "I have another reason for my visit. A marriage between our clans. I was hoping that Liam would meet Ella, yer sister. She is of marrying age is she not?"

"Ella is with the Macdonalds and will not return any time soon," Darach replied noncommittally. "Marriage between our clans is a conversation for another day."

"What of ye, Stuart?" the laird said pinning him with a smug look. "My daughter Lila is in need of a good match."

Stuart glanced at Darach before responding. "Like my brother stated, I believe this to be a conversation for another day."

"I do not have many days left," the Maclean barked. "I must resolve many matters before departing. Yer clan would be a good ally to ours. If my stubborn son would just take responsibility and do what is required, I would not have to be here. It should be he ensuring my last wishes are granted."

"Yer last wish—if I remember correctly—was for me to murder yer brother." Lennox stood at the doorway. With an expression of disgust, he met his father's gaze. "I will return, but only after worms are feasting on yer flesh."

If the pronouncement affected the Maclean, it was not noticeable. Obviously, such words had been exchanged before.

Liam however was not adept at hiding his emotions. "Ye are an embarrassment. Are not fit to be laird over our people."

Lennox's right eyebrow arched. "And a murderer is?"

There was a stunned silence. Everyone in the room waited to hear what would be said next. Stuart was riveted to the spot. What was happening before him was not unlike how things had been when his father lived. The late Ross was a hateful evil man, who turned people against one another for sport.

When he looked to Darach, he saw that his brother also seemed enthralled by the argument.

"Can we have some privacy please?" the Maclean asked, seeming to deflate at realizing they were witnessing a very personal argument.

Darach motioned to his personal guards to follow. "Aye." They all walked out.

Once out of earshot, Darach looked over his shoulder toward his study. "I hope to never become like him," Darach said, shaking his head. "Do ye think power does that to a man?"

"No, I do not believe so," Stuart replied. "Power makes whoever ye are grow. If a man is fair, then his fairness multiplies. If a man is evil…" He looked toward the library.

"I agree," Duncan said placing a hand on Darach's shoulder. "Ye are a good laird and will continue to be."

"As long as ye do not direct that I marry his daughter then all is well." Stuart shuddered.

They entered the great hall where servants scurried about setting out cups and plates for last meal.

Cait walked by carrying a tray laden with cups, a soft smile on her face as she chatted with a lad who walked alongside her carrying a large pitcher.

Following her progress, Stuart wondered what it would be like to have a conversation with her in which she'd smile like that at him.

"Mother seems to think ye are smitten with the lass." Darach gave him a long wink.

To his utter dismay, his cheeks heated. "Are ye going to ask her if she likes me?" he replied in a flat tone.

"She is quite bonnie," Duncan said. "Have ye spoken to her?"

"Are we lads again?" Stuart snapped. "We should be speaking of what is happening in yer study." Stuart tried to change the subject.

However, his brothers had found a weakness and were enjoying his discomfort too much.

"I think ye should speak to her now," Darach challenged.

"Who?" Gideon asked walking up. "Who should speak to whom?"

Duncan motioned to Cait who was placing cups at the high board. "Stuart to her."

"The lovely Cait," Gideon said in a hushed tone. "She is not one to take lightly. I must remind ye that her stepbrother is quite an able warrior."

"Ah, yes, Torac. He is rather large. But ye can take him," Darach said goading Stuart further.

Just then Cait turned, her eyes widened at the men staring at her. Stuart almost burst out laughing at his brothers being caught.

Darach cleared his throat. "We should go speak in the parlor." He turned on his heel and stalked from the room, Duncan and Gideon followed behind.

Stuart chuckled and went to her. "Forgive my brothers. Sometimes they revert to young lads when admiring a beautiful lass."

It was as if he told her she was about to be killed. The color drained from her face and her eyes bulged.

"Oh, goodness." She shoved the tray into his midsection and ran from the room.

He took two steps forward and then realizing he was holding an empty tray he handed it to the lad who gave him a curious look. "Go see about continuing yer duties," he said and went after Cait.

He found her in the servant's garden area. It wasn't really a garden, but a place where the people who worked for his family went to rest.

Upon seeing him a pair of chambermaids scurried back into the house.

Cait stood with her arms crossed looking in the direction of where the archery competition had taken place earlier.

Unsure of how to approach, he watched as she wiped at her cheeks with both hands and then crossed her arms again.

"Cait," he said approaching. Stuart did not like it one bit

when she stiffened. "I did not mean to scare or upset ye."

She nodded but did not look at him.

"I mean it. We did not mean any harm by it. I should not have said anything as I do not wish to make ye uncomfortable in yer duties."

"What do ye mean by my duties?" The words were soft.

"What I mean is yer duties—yer only duties—are whatever Greer decides."

He was in no way prepared for the fire emanating from her pretty eyes when she whirled to face him. With a solid stance, her feet planted, and arms bent at the elbow, she looked as if ready to fight.

"I will only give myself to the man I marry. If ye or yer brothers intend bedsport, ye must look elsewhere. Otherwise, I will leave immediately."

She made to go around him, and Stuart instinctively took her arm. She didn't recoil but may as well have from the way she looked at where his hand touched her.

"Ye misunderstand," he said. "Neither I nor my brothers would ever disrespect a woman in such a manner. Even Gideon—who I concede is a rogue—is approached by willing women, not the other way around. That is not our nature. I swear."

When she let out a breath, he released her arm and said, "I should not have shared what I did with ye. I was not thinking."

Cait's eyes were bright with unshed tears when she looked at him. "I do not know how to respond. Perhaps I was rash to have come to that conclusion. It is just that I have never lived in a keep before and Mother warned me that men, both the family and the guards, often take advantage of the servants who work here."

"She was right to warn ye," Stuart said. "I want to assure ye that we strive to ensure everyone within Ross keep is treated fairly and feels safe."

"It was not always so," she said. Obviously, she'd spoken to those who worked there prior to his father's death.

He shook his head. "No, it was not always so. It is my hope that things are very different from before. Darach often reminds the men who live here that the rules have changed."

"I apologize," she said in a quivering voice. "If ye wish me to go, I will."

"Of course not," he blurted. "Ye will remain here. I insist."

After a moment, she nodded.

"May I go now? There is much to do. Greer must be wondering where I am. I have duties to complete before going home."

Stuart fought to come up with a way to spend more time with her, but he could not think of what to say. "Aye. I look forward to whatever delicious dish Greer prepares."

"Pork and peas," she replied with a soft smile.

Something in his chest fluttered. The fact he wanted to ensure she was safe from anyone wishing to bring her harm became very important.

"The visitor is keeping us all quite busy," he said in a poor attempt at small talk.

Shouts sounded from the direction of the study.

"I best go," he touched her arm once more. "Again, I apologize."

"There is no need." Cait gave him a reassuring smile and his stomach did strange things.

THE MACLEAN AND his sons were obviously arguing. Stuart did not interfere but walked past to find his brothers.

When he entered the parlor, his brothers looked up with questioning looks but didn't say anything.

"What have we decided to do?" Stuart asked, not willing to speak about Cait.

"I will speak to both Lennox and the Maclean separately," Darach said. "I instructed the guard outside the door of my study to wait for Lennox to walk out, so he could be brought here."

At a loud shout, they all looked to the doorway. "They do not seem to be coming to an amenable arrangement," Duncan remarked.

"It is good that ye speak to Lennox," Stuart said to Darach. "Ye both have much in common. Our father's death was quick, it made it easier for ye, I suppose."

His brother's countenance changed, there was a slight sneer on his upper lip when he spoke. "His death was not fast enough."

Despite the grim statement, or perhaps because of it, Duncan chuckled. "The bastard did enough damage to last several lifetimes."

The sound of voices neared and moments later Lennox Maclean walked in. He was devoid of all expression. It was as if a ghost of the man who'd walked into the study now stood before Darach.

His gaze was flat, his face drawn. Letting out a breath, he neared and held out his hand. "I am returning to Skye. I cannot thank ye enough for everything."

Stuart and Duncan started to leave, but Darach stopped

them. “I need for ye both to hear this.”

“Join me for a moment.” Darach motioned to two chairs while Stuart poured Darach and Lennox a drink.

His brother met Lennox’s gaze for a long moment. “Ye return in order to save someone from harm I take it.”

Lennox nodded. “He gives me no choice. I fear he will mistreat others because of me. If I can ask one thing . . . Will ye allow the men to remain? It is not safe for them to return until after I am laird.”

“They can remain,” Darach said without hesitation.

“Who is in peril?” Stuart asked giving Lennox a glass of whiskey.

“Our family is filled with many secrets. If I were to speak of one, it would be easy to continue to tell of more.” Lennox swallowed the amber liquid. “I must return and speak to my men. We leave in the morning.”

“I took over this clan from a man whom I detested,” Darach began. “Thankfully, I have five brothers who have stood with me and given me the support I have needed throughout. Without them, I am not sure I would have succeeded. Speak to yer brother, ask him to be yer right hand.”

“Liam is bitter,” Lennox said. “It is hard for him to accept his lack of any power.”

“Then give him some,” Darach said. “Not only did I split the lands with my brothers, but each chose what they wanted to have as their primary duty. Ewan and Stuart are the best archers in the land. They are responsible for the recruitment, training, and command of our archers.”

He motioned to Duncan. “Duncan takes my place as laird whenever I go away. If he does not stand in for me, then Stuart or Caelan does."

Lennox leaned forward ensuring to hear each word Darach said.

"Our half brother, Caelan, shares our southern estate and lands with Duncan. He attended impressive schools in the lowlands and has a head for numbers. Caelan controls the finances and oversees the clan ledgers. Our youngest brother, Gideon, is still learning his way. For now, he is a scout and warrior."

"What stops any of them from attempting to take yer place as laird?" Lennox asked looking from Darach to Stuart and then to Duncan.

His brother's lips curved. "Each other, I suppose. If my brothers decided to oust me, I will have to presume it would be for good reason."

"I do not know if I have as much trust in my brothers. There is another, Lachlan, he is third-born."

"Yer parents had an affinity for the letter L?" Stuart asked.

"It would seem," Lennox replied with a soft smile. "We are each named after ancestors."

"Are ye sure to return then?" Darach asked.

"Aye, I must. It is my duty to the clan," Lennox replied. "My father has requested a meal in his bedchamber."

Darach motioned to Duncan. "My brother and I can spend some time after last meal with ye and answer any questions ye may have."

"I cannot thank ye enough. That ye do not resent that I did not divulge who I was makes me respect ye even more."

# CHAPTER FIVE

WHEN THE STRAP of her knapsack became uncomfortable, Cait moved it to her other shoulder, as she trudged through the forest toward home. Knowing she had a long walk home after her duties were completed, Greer always did her best to allow Cait to leave as soon as last meal was served.

Fall was approaching and the weather was quite chilly that day. Pulling her shawl tighter around her shoulders, she quickened her pace, ready to be inside the warmth of home. But at the sound of leaves rustling, she froze and listened. The snorts of a boar made her blood run cold. She'd run into wild animals before on her daily treks to and from the keep, but thankfully never a boar.

After a moment, except for the wind sifting through the trees, the woods were once again silent. Just as she decided it was safe to resume her walk home, a boar and her two piglets appeared in the path. Cait wasn't sure what to do. If the animal considered her a threat to her young, she would not hesitate to attack. In hopes the animal would continue on its way, Cait took two steps sideways and stood behind a tree.

Just then someone whistled a strange tune. One high shrill whistle followed by two short lower pitched ones. Whoever it was seemed to be in a good mood. Cait moved around the tree so now she was out of view from both the boar and whoever approached. This was turning out to be quite an annoying walk home.

A horseman came into view. Whoever it was allowed his steed to meander at a leisurely pace. When he whistled again, she peeked around the tree. It was Stuart Ross.

"Ugh," he said, and she knew he'd seen the boar.

"Go away Mother and take yer young with ye. I do not wish to hurt ye."

There were snorts from the boar's direction. Obviously, the animal was not happy at the appearance of a horse.

Stuart held his horse still and moments later the boar continued on. The piglets squealing as they trotted after their disgruntled mother.

"I went to the kitchens to find ye and offer ye a ride to yer home. But Greer told me ye had already left," Stuart called out.

Cait came from behind the tree. "Thank ye, but I do not require it." She did her best to keep her expression stern. Although, in truth, she was relieved that he'd scared the boar away. There was no telling how long she would have had to hide behind the tree before the animal decided to leave.

"Many animals give birth during the late summer. Which means ye will have encounters with protective mothers all season. Ye should consider riding a horse home," Stuart informed her.

Crossing her arms, Cait gave him a blank look. "I do not have a horse, Mister Stuart. Furthermore, I have never ridden one." She turned on her heel and began walking.

Stuart dismounted and walked alongside, pulling his horse behind. "We must remedy that at once. Ye should have asked my brother for a horse. He would have given ye one."

"Yer brother gives away horses to anyone who asks?"

He shook his head. "I meant the use of a horse. The animal would belong to our family. Unless ye bought it, or it was gifted to ye. I am not aware if he has given away horses. I shall ask him."

"Why would ye and yer brother offer a horse for me to ride?" Cait was incredulous. The more she spoke to Stuart, the more confused she became over what to think of the Ross family. Did they treat all the servants so kindly? She recalled that Lady Isobel often spent time in the kitchen with Greer. Both Lady Isobel and Lady Mariel's companions spent time with the family and not the servants.

However, this was totally different. Had Stuart followed her?

"Ye confuse me," she finally replied. "Why are ye here?" She scanned the woods realizing they were alone and if the man decided to have his way with her, there was little she could do. At the same time, there was something about him that made her feel at ease. It was as if instinctively she knew he would not hurt her.

"I do not mean to. What if I give ye lessons?"

"What?"

"I can teach ye to ride a horse."

"I do not wish to be up so high on an animal on my own."

"'Tis easy."

Cait blew out a breath. "I appreciate yer offer but must refuse it."

"Come. Let us ride to yer home. We can discuss this another day." He took her arm and guided her over to his now still horse then lifted her up into the saddle. After settling Cait, he deftly mounted and with arms on both sides of her, he took the reins and maneuvered the horse forward.

Astride the horse, she ensured her skirts covered her legs. It felt strange to be up so high from the ground and she didn't quite care for it.

"I have no idea where ye live, so ye will have to tell me," Stuart said, his mouth much too close to her ear. "Here, take the reins." He placed the leather straps into her hands, then put his hands over hers so she could see how he guided the horse. After a while, he released her hands and allowed her to guide the horse alone.

"Ye are assisting with yer legs are ye not?" Cait asked. It was a strange feeling to be sitting so close to him; her backside between his open legs touching the most private part of him. At the same time, he continued to put her at ease. He didn't try to pull her closer and somehow managed to keep from touching her.

"I am," he replied. "That will be a lesson I can only give ye when ye are on the horse by yerself."

She gave up trying to explain that she had no intention of ever learning to ride a horse.

When she motioned to the small cottage that was her home, he took the reins and guided the horse the rest of the way. Upon arriving, both his mother and brother hurried out. Her mother looked up at them with eyes wide with worry.

"Is something wrong? Were ye injured?"

"Nothing is wrong," Cait replied suddenly unsure what to do.

Stuart dismounted and helped her down. He went to her

mother. “I am Stuart Ross. There are many wild boars with young in the woods right now, so I ensured yer daughter did not come to any harm.”

“I see,” her mother had lowered into a slight curtsy upon him divulging who he was. But now looked at him with distrust. “Her half brother should feel obligated to see to her safety.”

“Torac barely speaks to me,” Cait said. “I assured Mister Stuart that I am perfectly capable of traveling back and forth on my own.”

Brice walked closer, his young face stern. “I can walk her to the keep and then meet her upon the end of her day to walk her back home.”

“A horse can be supplied for Cait to travel back and forth. Once she leans to ride, it will make things easier,” Stuart insisted giving her a pointed look.

“We cannot afford to feed and care for the laird’s horse,” her mother said with a worried expression. “Mister Stuart, ye must understand . . . we have meager means. Cait provides what we have.”

Cait wanted to tell her mother to stop speaking, but she bit her bottom lip. It wasn’t as if her mother lied.

“That is true, we could not afford the feed. I do thank ye for the offer; however, as I said before, I must decline,” Cait told him.

“I am sure something can be done to keep ye from harm.” He looked to the cottage and then met her brother’s gaze. “Ye do good work. The cottage looks much better than the last time I saw it.”

Her brother beamed with pride. The two walked to the

back so that Brice could show Stuart where he was adding a room.

"What is he expecting in return for all of this attention?" her mother whispered. "Did he make any untoward advances?"

Cait shook her head. "No, Mother. I would have jumped from the horse, and we would have left immediately if something like that had happened."

Her mother gave her a sad look. "And where would we go child?"

"I would find a way for us," Cait replied with much more resolution than she felt. The resignation in her mother's face told her that if one of the Ross brothers ever decided to take her, it would probably be something she'd not have any choice but to accept.

"I am assured more and more each day that they are good and decent people," she finally said as Stuart came from behind the house.

He gave them a nod, then mounted and rode away. Once again whistling the strange two tones.

Turning away and heading for the house, she and her mother went straight to the kitchen. From the knapsack, she took out the leftover duck and a pair of turnips she'd taken from the garden with Greer's permission. After chopping the turnips and the duck meat, it was all put into a pot of water boiling over the fire. Along with bread her mother had baked earlier in the day, it would be a simple meal as always, but thankfully, they'd be quite full.

The next morning Cait did not go to the keep. Greer had given her two days' rest, which she was extremely grateful for.

There was clothing to mend and wash, and she wanted to spend some time taking in a dress and underskirts that she'd gotten when Lady Ross had offered a pile of clothes for the maids to choose from.

Her mother studied her while she swept the floors. "If ye married, then I would have less to worry about."

Cait stopped mid-sweep. "Who would ye have me marry Mother?"

"I know there are plenty of guardsmen at the keep. One or two have surely taken yer attention."

In truth, she'd been much too busy to pay attention to any men. Between her duties in the kitchen and serving in the great hall—not to mention her long treks back and forth from home to the keep to home again—there was little time for frivolity.

She'd never admit to her mother how tired she was most days and what little amount of time there was to even consider things like courtship. There was a maid or two that she'd noted had relationships, but she'd not been at the keep long enough to keep up with who was with whom.

"Consider it," her mother continued. "Then ye and he could ride home together and the men at the keep would stay at arm's length. Even the roguish ones will stay away from a married lass. Ye are much too pretty not to be protected."

Cait laughed. "Truly Mother, ye should not fret over it. We will be well. I have two brothers to ensure it."

"Once we save enough for a mule and I build a cart, I can take ye to the keep in the mornings and retrieve ye after," Brice interjected. "Though I do hope we get a horse," he added wistfully.

Their mother gave him a pointed look. "Do not go making such plans," she said. "We cannot possibly accept it. How would we feed it?"

"It is true, we cannot accept such a gift," Cait interjected. "I am truly sorry Brice, I know ye wish to work. Ye are too young to seek labor yet. We need ye here for now."

Her brother shrugged good-naturedly. "I have plenty to keep me busy here."

She considered her conversation with Stuart Ross about her brother. "What would ye like to do one day. If given the choice?"

"Work in the stables. And one day have my own corral full of horses," Brice replied without hesitation. "Ye could accept the horse. I will find ways to feed it. I wish to learn about them."

When he gave her one of his wistful looks, it was hard to resist. "Perhaps when ye get older, ye can work at the stables. Then we can ask to live at the keep." Changing the subject, she smiled at him. "For now, I'll see if I can borrow a cart and mule so we can venture to the village."

That brightened her mother and her brother, who both gave her thankful looks.

The next two days flew past. She accomplished everything and was prepared to return to work, well rested. It was Greer's habit to give servants a few days off every other month, to keep them from growing weary. Other than that, they could take a day off every fortnight.

On the day she was to return to work she was already heading through the woods towards the keep at sunrise. Aware of the breeding animals, she was careful to keep her attention sharp as to not miss any sounds or sights.

At the sound of the two-toned whistle, she blew out a breath. The man was relentless. Why was Stuart Ross so intent on seeking her out? If as he said, he had no intention of anything untoward.

Moments later, the huge warhorse appeared through the trees. With a quiver of arrows strapped to his broad back and dark hair flying across his face, he looked like a god descended from the clouds. A god of war and destruction.

"Ah, there ye are," he said in a pleasant tone as if she should have been expecting him. "I came to fetch ye for work. Greer is most put out this morning as Finella is not feeling well and Cora is nowhere to be found."

Cora was in a relationship with one of the guardsmen. However, Cait was not about to say anything about it.

"Did Greer ask ye to seek me out?" Cait asked allowing herself to be hoisted up to sit on the horse.

He shook his head. "I told her I was going hunting and that I might run into ye. She then asked if I didn't mind hurrying ye along if I did see ye."

"Actually, I am glad to have a moment to speak to ye," Cait started in a tone she hoped conveyed assurance. "Please do not insist on treating me differently than the other servants. I do not wish to be singled out. It could lead to talk that would be most unkind."

"I have something to show ye when we get to the keep."

"Impossible," Cait argued. "As ye yerself intimated, Greer needs me immediately."

He shrugged and she realized she was leaning her shoulder on him. Cait immediately straightened putting space between them.

The feel of his body against hers made Cait's heart speed and she soon found it was becoming hard to breathe normally.

"Is something wrong?" Stuart asked, which both annoyed and angered her. It would be so embarrassing to feel the way she did about a man so above her station. That he paid her attention made it even worse. To allow her heart hope was both cruel and sobering.

Stuart pulled the horse to a stop and dismounted. "Come," he said holding his arms out. "Whatever is wrong, ye need to relax a bit."

Cait blew out a breath and closed her eyes. "I should walk the rest of the way."

When he helped her down Stuart held her still, his eyes on her face assessing if she was unwell.

To her horror, he closed the distance between them and pressed his lips to hers. To make matters worse, she clung to his shoulders letting out a sigh when the kiss deepened.

The kiss was like nothing she ever imagined. His mouth exploring hers: suckling, teasing, tasting. Responding with like motions, her hands slid up from his shoulders to his strong jaw.

"I have wanted to kiss ye since the first time I saw ye," he murmured between kisses.

With one last press against her lips, he straightened and smiled down at her. "Do ye feel better?"

Worse. She felt worse.

"We…we should not have done that."

"I think we should have," he replied lifting her back onto the horse.

Her mind raced in all directions as they neared the keep. What had she done? Why had she responded with so much enthusiasm?

She closed her eyes, grateful to have her back to him. Did this mean he would expect more from her? Her body perhaps. She swallowed at the thought of what to do next.

"Stop thinking," he murmured. "It was a kiss, that is all. I have no expectations from ye."

Cait blew out a breath. "Good."

"Ye wound my heart," he replied good-naturedly and despite all the trepidations, Cait smiled. Stuart Ross was a most perplexing man.

UPON ENTERING THE gates, she was thankful only a few people were about. "Please help me down. I must go inside with haste."

He dismounted and lowered her to the ground. "Come along. I have something to show ye."

"Hold him here, I will return shortly," Stuart told a lad, handing him the reins. Then he stalked toward the stables, Cait almost running to keep up with his long strides.

Finally, they came to the stables and he went directly to a stall. Inside was a beautiful tan and white mare. The animal was delicate and seemed sweet.

"She is to be yers. Darach purchased it for Isobel, but Lady Ross prefers large, strong horses. So, this mare has been lingering without someone to ride her."

Cait reached out and ran her hand down the horse's long nose. Then she instinctively caressed the animal's jawline. The mare made a happy grunting noise.

"Ye are a natural," Stuart said with a smile. "Ensure to tell Greer ye have riding lessons today right after midday meal."

"No," Cait stated firmly. "I will not."

With a good-natured shrug, he turned and walked away.

As she arrived at the kitchen entrance, she saw Stuart galloping away to his hunting grounds.

Greer clapped her hands upon Cait entering. "Bless Mister Stuart for fetching ye. I am going to scold Cora once she appears, for not being here this morning. Poor Finella does not have the strength to get out of bed." Greer bustled from one simmering pot to frying sounds from a flat pan over the fire.

"See about the plates and fetch the pitchers," Greer told a maid who'd entered, effectively sending the girl rushing away. Greer was always especially stern with the younger maids. She'd told Cait it was mainly because if she wasn't they'd begin lazy and stay that way.

It was a long while later that just as Cait hoisted a tray of food up, Cora hurried into the room.

Cait gave her a warning look and Cora gave her a soft nod of acknowledging she was prepared to be scolded. She blew out a breath and walked to where Greer waited with both her hands on her hips.

"Where 'ave ye gotten off too?"

Once the people in the great hall were served, she and Cora continued to refill tankards, while lads hurried about removing platters and such.

"I must tell ye something," Cora said when they went to refill their pitchers. "I was with Torac."

"I wasn't sure it was my brother who courted ye." Cait was troubled that her brother had not spoken to her in as many days.

Cora grinned. “I wish to get to know him better. What can ye tell me?”

It was astounding that Cora stole away with a man and knew little about him. “I do not know my half brother well. There is little free time, as ye know.”

Placing the last empty pitcher in the kitchen, Cait picked up two buckets. “I will go fetch water,” she said over her shoulder and walked outside.

The person she sought was standing with legs apart, sword in hand, slicing through the air in a pattern. Back and forth he swung, sweat glistening across his brow.

“Torac,” Cait said nearing. “I must speak to ye.”

Her brother glowered in her direction, his gaze moving past her. “What is it?”

Once he lowered the sword, she neared. Not that she expected him to hurt her, but she wasn’t sure how to approach someone who was so intent on training. “Cora told me ye are courting her.”

His handsome face scrunched into a frown. “Did she now?”

“I am sure ye plan to marry the lass. Especially since Greer had everyone search for her and could not find her in her quarters.” Cait met his gaze with a pointed look. “I am sure speculations are beginning.”

The expressions of worry that crossed Torac’s face made her want to giggle. Before he could say anything, she spoke again. “How old does one have to be to train with horses? Brice is interested but I am worried about our mother being left alone all day.”

It was a moment before Torac was able to tear his gaze from the direction of the kitchen. "Ah…I suppose he is old enough. Why do ye bring it up, if ye do not wish him to be away from yer home?"

"I do not want to hold him back either. I ask so that we can make a decision about it."

Torac nodded. "Once he is ready, I will ensure he has a place at the stables. Understand that he will have to live in the rooms there and will not go home daily. Apprentices often are the ones who handle the horses at night."

"I can ask Lady Isobel for a room in the servant's quarters and share with Mother, I suppose."

"Ensure Brice is ready. Once he comes, he cannot simply walk away."

"I will." She gave him a soft smile. "Cora is lovely."

His eyes narrowed, not giving Cait a good feeling.

"One last thing, can ye acquire a mule and cart for a day? It would be helpful to take Mother to the village when I have a day of rest."

Her brother met her gaze. "I can see about one for ye to use."

# CHAPTER SIX

WHEN STUART RETURNED from hunting, it was still early in the day. He'd given up after only a couple of hours, his mind much too involved in rethinking the kiss with Cait. Like a lad, he returned to the keep hoping to catch a glimpse of her.

Once he dismounted, he saw her. She was with another servant, both carrying water toward the kitchen.

She looked toward him, her cheeks turned pink, and she turned away.

When spotting her brother, Stuart went to him and told him about his idea to gift Cait the mare.

"A horse?" Torac asked giving him a curious look and then glancing in the direction that Cait went.

"She walks a long distance to and from the cottage. Yesterday, I was hunting and came upon her hiding from a boar. I told her we could allow her the use of a horse."

The warrior narrowed his eyes. "She does not require a horse, Mister Stuart. Cait can walk, or I can see about a mule and cart."

Not wishing to continue the discussion with her half brother, who obviously cared little about Cait's welfare, Stuart shrugged. "Let us practice."

There was little doubt left in his mind that Torac was not

upset about the horse, but about the fact that Stuart had noticed his sister. By the time they finished sparing, not only was Stuart drenched in sweat, but there had been a couple of times he'd wondered if the man meant to kill him.

"Point taken," he told the warrior, who gave him one last glare and stalked away.

At the water barrel, he dipped a bowl into the cold water and poured it over his head. Then repeated the process, washing as much dirt and sweat as he could before going inside.

"What was that about?" Darach neared and gave him a questioning look. "Are ye fighting over a woman?"

"Was it that obvious?" Stuart asked watching his brother wash up. "I do not think he cares that I pay attention to his sister."

Darach chuckled. "I do not have to ask who the fair lass is. What do ye plan to do?"

The question caught him off guard. For the moment, the only thing he'd planned was to teach her to ride so that she'd have a way back and forth from the cottage in the woods. Now he worried it would cause a problem between him and Torac.

"I do not know," he replied. "The cottage ye gave her family is much too far and her trudging through the woods in the early morn and late eve is dangerous."

His brother chuckled and shook his head. "I suppose ye should do something about it then. There is no need for the wee wench to be in any danger." When his brother walked away chuckling, Stuart visualized throwing the water bowl at the back of his head.

He walked past the garden then took a step back when he

noticed Cait digging at the dirt with a small spade. She hummed as she worked not noticing him.

It was time to stop the foolishness. He'd made sure she had a way to and from the cottage. He would arrange for someone else to teach her. The last thing he needed was any kind of complications in his life. There was much to do with archer training duties and plans for rotation of the guards at the northern and southern posts.

Soon, he and his team of archers, along with a group of warriors, would be going to the southern shore to replace those on guard there.

"Cait," he called out much louder than he intended.

When Cait saw him, her eyes rounded. She attempted to stand but stepped on something and lost her balance falling backward onto the ground.

Blowing out soft breaths, she remained on her bottom with her head bent.

"I did not mean to startle ye," Stuart said as he neared. When she didn't move, he noticed that she held her right hand in her left, blood seeping through her fingers.

"Here let me help." He grabbed her by the shoulders and lifted her to stand.

Cait let out a shaky breath. "It hurts."

Stuart walked her to the water barrel and once again dipped the bowl into it, then washed the wound. It was a deep cut that would need to be stitched. The bleeding did not stop, but at least all the dirt was gone.

"Come inside, Mother can help."

Pale and looking as if she was fighting not to cry, the lass allowed him to guide her to the great hall. He called out for a servant to fetch his mother and almost immediately his mother hurried to them. "Oh, dear, what happened?"

"I startled her, and she cut herself with the garden spade," Stuart explained. "It was not my intention. I thought she'd seen me."

"Poor lass," his mother said. At the words, his brother's wife, Isobel, arrived and pushed him away.

"Please fetch my kit from the shelf there." She pointed to a cabinet by the corridor. Stuart did as Isobel instructed.

"Stuart, hold her still. The cut is long, and this will hurt." Isobel gave Cait an apologetic look. "If ye have to cry, it's fine Cait."

Stuart pulled up a chair and sat behind Cait. He held her against his chest. The lass shivered and he knew she was in great pain. The cut went from between her thumb and forefinger to the other side of her hand. It was an awful place for a jagged cut, and he knew it would cause her discomfort for a long time.

At the first stitch Cait cried out softly, and her breathing became more irregular with each subsequent one. Each time the needle pierced her skin, Stuart ached for her.

"I am so very sorry," he kept repeating in her ear. Whether she heard him over the pain, he wasn't sure.

By the time Isobel finished stitching her hand and wrapping it, Cait was sobbing.

"Why do ye cry?" his mother asked. "Does it continue to hurt lass?"

Cait sniffed loudly. "With my hand cut, I cannot continue to work and feed my family. Wh-what shall I do?"

"Do not worry about that right now," Isobel said.

Both women gave Stuart a disappointed look. Finally, he mouthed "What?"

"Tell Cait what ye plan to do to help?" his mother said giving him a wide-eyed look as if there was an obvious thing to say.

"I will get herbs that will help with the pain from Greer," he started and when his mother motioned with her hand for him to continue, he said, "And I will take ye home to rest."

By the roll of his mother's eyes and Isobel's head shake, he'd said the wrong thing.

"Ye should stay here where we can look after ye," Isobel said. "Stuart will also…" She looked to him.

Cait turned and met his gaze. His heart melted at seeing her wet eyelashes clumped together around her red-rimmed eyes. "I will inform yer mother what has happened and ensure that yer family has everything they need until ye can work again."

His mother's wide smile made it obvious he'd finally said the right thing.

LEAVING THE WOMEN to do whatever it was they did, Stuart went to find Anton. His squire nodded emphatically while he gave instructions for food and grain to be taken to Cait's home and a message that she would be unable to travel home for a few days.

Once that was completed, he sought Darach to discuss the upcoming changing of duties at the southern post. In the study he found his brothers, Darach, Ewan, and Gideon.

With his wife in the family way, Duncan had returned to his home and was not expected to return to the keep unless there was a good reason.

Ewan lived close enough that he could travel back and forth daily, so he was usually at the keep most of the day helping with whatever was needed.

"A messenger just arrived," Darach said. "Laird Maclean has died."

Stuart lowered to a chair. "He was right, he had only a few days left."

"The message also states that Lila Maclean may be visiting soon. I am sure it was one of the late laird's wishes that she marries well."

"She can marry Caelan then," Stuart said.

Darach arched a brow. "Ye were specified. I suppose the late Maclean expects ye not to have a problem moving to Skye."

"I would wait until seeing the lass before making up yer mind," Gideon said with eyebrows raised and a twist to his lips. "Do not agree to anything until ye see her, she may be homely."

"Looks are not what makes a marriage of convenience work," Ewan stated.

"Says the man who married a beauty," Gideon quipped. He then addressed Darach. "Do not ever consider marrying me off to someone I do not find attractive."

Their eldest brother shook his head. "I would never consider marrying anyone off, especially not ye Gideon. The poor woman who ends up with ye will have a life of misery trying to keep ye in line."

Everyone chuckled, except for Stuart. His mind was awhirl at the idea of a woman traveling there to meet him and that if he did agree to marry, he would leave his family and lands.

"Is there something to gain from an alliance between our clans?"

Darach nodded. "Possibly. However, I feel that Lennox will remain friendly because we gave him and his men harbor."

"Some of his men remain here as well," Gideon added. "Ye do not have to marry the lass unless ye wish to."

"Can we discuss the southern guard exchange?" Stuart said changing the subject. "What are the plans?"

"Gideon will go in yer place," Darach said.

The youngest nodded in agreement. "I will be an archer for a season."

"Why?" Stuart argued. "It is my turn to go."

"Ye must remain. If ye are gone when Lila Maclean arrives, it will be an affront to Lennox Maclean. He is newly laird and attempting to fulfill some of his father's last wishes."

"An arranged marriage? Honestly Darach, ye can send a message back telling him I will not marry her and save her the trip."

"Gideon, ensure the warriors are prepared to go in three days. Ewan, see about the archers," Darach ordered, not meeting his gaze. "See if our cousin, Artair, plans to go as well."

The others dispersed, but Stuart remained rooted to the chair. "I am not going to marry Lila Maclean."

Darach shrugged. "I am aware that ye are interested in the wee lass, Cait. If ye are serious about her, ye should make it known soon. Ye being betrothed will make things easier to keep from insulting the Maclean. Otherwise, ye will have to court the Maclean lass to see if ye are in fact compatible."

"I just startled Cait in the garden. She cut her hand and is not able to work. I do not believe this to be a good time to speak to her about courtship," he muttered. "Besides, her brother hates me."

Not looking to speak on the subject any longer, Darach stood. Pushing back from the chair, his brother pulled a rolled-up map from a shelf and flattened it on the table. They used cups and other items to the edges down.

"This area is not protected." Darach pointed to a western portion of their lands, just below the lands that belonged to Stuart. "Can ye and some men ride out there and scout it. I do not want to post men there permanently, but if it's a one-day ride there and back, we can add it to the patrol assignments."

"I will go first thing in the morning." Stuart noted that he'd ride past where Cait lived. It would be a good opportunity to bring any other needed provisions to her mother and brother.

HIS MOTHER MET him as he walked out of the study. "Ye should go speak to her." She motioned up the stairs.

If this was any indication of how courtship was to start, he wasn't sure to be very good at it. Stuart went up the stairs and knocked on the open door. When she called for him to enter, he found Cait sitting in a chair in front of the fireplace cradling her bandaged hand to her chest.

Just then Cora, one of the kitchen maids, entered and placed a cup on a small table next to where Cait sat.

"It hurts quite badly," she explained lifting her tear-streaked face.

"Greer says this will put ye right to sleep. It'll help with the pain too."

"I cannot stay here," Cait said looking to the other woman. "I will go back to the room in the servant's quarters. I do not understand why I am here." She began to cry, and Stuart looked to the servant motioning for her to leave.

The woman nodded in understanding and walked out.

"Drink the tea, it will help ye feel better."

CAIT WASN'T SURE what to do. Confused at the entire situation coupled with the throbbing pain made her want to kick and scream like a child and not really caring what anyone thought. Her head pounded and every single moment that passed seemed to increase the anxious feelings inside her chest.

When Stuart's hand cupped her jaw, it was as if everything stopped whirling. The warmth of his hand seeped into her skin and she leaned into it, closing her eyes.

He must have knelt, because when he pulled her against him, they were at the same level. Pushing away all thought, she rested her head on his shoulder.

"When I am in pain," he said in a low voice, "I force myself to drink whatever Greer concocts. It will be vile, but it always works."

His lips pressed to her neck, just below her left ear sending out tingles of awareness. "I do not know what I feel for ye Cait. But I must admit that ye are always on my mind."

The statement broke the spell and she attempted to straighten, but his arms tightened around her as he lifted her and carried her to the bed.

Cait's breath caught. Surely, he did not mean to take advantage of her injury and have his way with her. She wasn't sure she had the strength to do much more than continue crying.

Upon lowering her onto the soft bedding, he straightened and went back to fetch the cup that Cora had brought.

Holding it to her lips, he met her gaze. “Drink.”

She took a sip and cringed.

“I told ye it would be vile. ’Tis best to swallow it fast and do yer best to keep it down.”

Cait nodded and took the cup with her left hand. Because his gaze locked with hers, she barely noticed the horrible taste of the drink. Instead, she marveled at the fact that she—a mere servant—was getting so much attention from him.

“Now,” he said making Cait stiffen and wonder what would happen next. “I will kiss ye and leave ye to rest.”

True to his word, he bent down, pressed his lips to hers in a sweet lingering kiss, trailed kisses to her ear, then looked her in the eyes and order her to, “Rest.”

The door closed and she stared at it with fascination.

She slipped from the bed, slid her shoes on, and walked out. No matter how nice he was, she would maintain her dignity. It was not her place to have one of the guest rooms.

Cora caught sight of her when she stumbled groggily in the servant’s corridor. “What are ye doing? I thought ye to be sleeping by now.”

“I am seeking my bed,” she said stubbornly. “Mister Stuart feels responsible for my injury. Although it is partly true, there is no need to install me in a guest chamber.”

“Come along,” Cora said helping her walk to the small room that she kept at the keep. Once settled onto the slender bed, Cait fought to remain awake. “Be sure to come and fetch me so I can help as much as I can with last meal.”

When Cora left, Cait realized that Stuart's kisses had distracted her from the pain. Thankfully Greer's concoction was completing the task. And as her pain eased, her mind cleared, leaving her better able to decide what she needed to do.

One thing she knew for certain, she had to clarify things with Stuart. She had to make certain he understood that she could not leave her mother and younger brother on their own. They were *her* responsibility.

Of course, there was also the circumstances of their social stations. Although his family seemed to accept that there was the possibility of a relationship between them, Cait wasn't so sure. Her being so far below him is what led her to believe that—despite his assurances it wasn't true—he did not desire her for a relationship. He was just looking for a dalliance. And if she was right, she had to put a stop to any physical contact between them. Immediately.

Unfortunately, as her body continued to relax and her eyes drooped close her thoughts were filled with just how wonderful his kisses were.

THE NEXT MORNING, Stuart rose early to go to see about the western portion of Ross land as his brother had directed. He'd spent the majority of the last evening figuring a way out of his current predicament.

The entire idea of marriage as a way for clans to unite was one of the things he disliked about being part of the laird's family. Thankfully his brother was giving him the choice of who he married. He could only hope it wouldn't come to him having to marry someone else's choice as part of his duties to the clan.

As he and four guardsmen mounted their horses and prepared to ride, Artair rode up. "I hear ye are not going to the southern post." His cousin gave him a side glance before adding, "I am not going either."

"Why?"

"My father is ill. I prefer to remain close by." Artair brought his mount alongside his as they headed out of the keep.

"I wasn't aware Uncle Angus was unwell. Why has no one told us?"

Artair shook his head. "We did not think it was serious. But it seems to linger. The healer is seeing to him."

They rode for a while in silence until reaching the cottage where Cait's mother and brother lived. Both came out as soon as he rode up.

"Did something happen to Cait?" Her mother looked up at him, her face pale and filled with worry. "Why is she not with ye?"

Stuart explained about Cait cutting her hand—leaving out his part in the incident—and after giving them a basket Greer had prepared and reassuring the woman her daughter was well, he and Artair continued on their way.

"Ye seem to know them and the daughter well," his cousin said. "Is there something between ye and the lass?"

Stuart watched a hawk fly overhead. Its wings spread with the concise fluidity of a predator that spotted its prey. The bird let out a piercing warning call, as if to warn of its plan before diving behind the trees.

"I do not wish for any romantic entanglements at the moment. However, Lennox Maclean seems determined to follow through with his late father's wishes. They hated each other, so it came as quite a surprise when he sent a message stating that his sister Lila is to come for a visit."

Artair blew out a breath. "And ye are the one who's been chosen as suitor?"

"Aye."

"I do not blame ye for not wishing to be involved. I will never marry. I do not agree with the idea of it. Especially not an arranged one."

Stuart let the comment go. Ever since they were children, Artair made statements with a certainty that no one questioned. Even if he didn't follow through, he always maintained a sort of formality about him. It was what kept Stuart and his brothers from pointing out when Artair did not see something through.

They'd barely ridden out of the forest when men on horseback burst from the trees; their swords lifted. Both he and Artair drew theirs just in time to defend against the attackers.

He had no time to try to identify who they were as they battled against the group of men. Despite the four guardsmen rushing forward to assist, they were still outnumbered.

His and Artair's horses circled as trained while they swung their swords. The sounds of metal against metal echoing through the trees.

Stuart fought against two men, who seemed intent on separating him from the others. Tiring, he fought to lift the heavy sword and lean into his swings. The men kept their distance, not coming close enough for him to reach past their sword.

A swoosh sounded as one of the men struck his hand and his sword flew from it. Unarmed, Stuart jumped down from his horse and dashed to the protection of the forest. Just before he reached the trees, a hard blow to the back of his head sent him sprawling to the ground.

Then everything went black.

# CHAPTER SEVEN

THE FIRST THING Stuart wanted to do was retch upon waking. His stomach heaved and he gagged. The swaying under him meant he traveled on water. He attempted to sit up but being bound made it impossible.

"I am about to be sick," he told the closest man, who stood and grabbed him by the back of his tunic and roughly dragged him to the side of the bìrlinn.

The combination of nausea and his hatred of being at sea made him furious. He threw up until he was sure his next heave would send out his stomach. The continued movement of the boat made him want to jump into the water and drown himself.

"For a man who lives on the isles, I am shocked that ye are not a seafarer," the man said.

He recognized the voice. It was Ethan, one of the Uisdein's sons.

"What in the devil do ye want with me?" he snapped. "Did the lesson after imprisoning Darach not teach yer father anything?"

"Father wishes to see ye. I am bringing ye to finish what ye started."

The blood in his veins turned cold. "What exactly do ye mean?"

"Ye and my sister are betrothed. Ye must marry her."

Falling back, Stuart began to laugh. In turn, heaving and laughing until he felt delirious.

"What is so funny," the Uisdein's son asked.

"I-I cannot marry them all." Stuart could not stop laughing. "Can I have three wives?"

Ethan glared. "What nonsense are ye spewing?"

He sobered and glared at the man. "I will not marry Flora. Yer father is who broke off the betrothal. What has changed?"

"Ye do not know anything," he responded bluntly. "Ye will marry her as soon as we arrive."

The trip to the Isle of Benbecula was not long, perhaps a pair of hours. Stuart mentally timed how long it would take for Artair, or one of the guardsmen, to make it back to the keep—if they'd survived.

"What happened to my men?"

Ethan shrugged. "None were killed if that is what ye wish to know. We are not barbarians."

"No, that is not the reason ye did not kill them. It is because ye fear my brother's wrath." Once again Stuart chuckled. "Ye underestimate him if ye think he willna come after ye with all his fury."

Because of the seasickness, the short trip seemed to take much longer. Of all his brothers, he was the only one that got sick when on a boat. Despite it, he was not glad to see the shoreline.

Once they came ashore, Ethan ordered that his hands be untied. Horses waited on the shore. Stuart mounted, eager to get the confrontation over with. When Ethan gave him a suspicious look, he hitched an eyebrow. "Let us go and see what yer father hopes to accomplish."

Ethan grunted but did not reply.

The Uisdein was a pampered egotistical man, with little sense. Stuart prayed he'd find a way to talk himself out of this predicament before anything permanent occurred.

It was not Stuart's first time visiting the isle. Several times he'd accompanied his father, who for some reason wished an alliance with the Uisdein.

Part of the agreement was for him to marry the Uisdein's daughter, Flora. At the time, it had been a surprise to Stuart and the lass.

Apparently, his father had not chosen Darach, as he hoped for a more beneficial match for him. Duncan could not be forced to do anything, and Ewan was gone. That just left him. He was given no say in the matter.

Although he had come to care deeply for Flora, now all he felt was contempt. Not only for the Uisdein who'd abruptly broken the agreement, but for his daughter who he'd been told had decided to marry someone else.

If Flora was in love with someone else, it was understandable. At the same time, he often wondered why she'd initiated intimacy between them.

His stomach had yet to settle so he breathed deeply in an effort to be in a good frame of mind once coming face to face with people he never thought to see again.

They passed through the gates into a small but well-tended courtyard. Once there, he dismounted and was shoved forward into the main house.

He entered flanked by Ethan and another man.

"Stuart Ross, I am pleased at yer appearance."

The Uisdein made a show of waving him in. Sitting at the high board in a chair that would be best suited for a king, the laird looked down at him.

At Stuart remaining silent, the man continued, "There is much to do and little time. I am sure yer brother and his army of warriors will arrive soon. Therefore, this marriage must be completed immediately."

"Are ye mad?" Stuart asked.

The laird glared at him. "No, ye are the one who is mad to think ye can stand up to me. I am Laird Uisdein." He motioned around the room to guards that stood at a ready. "I will not stand for disrespect from another Ross."

"I am not going to marry yer daughter."

"Where is Flora," the Uisdein asked, clapping his hands. "Tell her to come at once. It is time."

A maid ran across the room, tripped on her skirts, and fell to the floor, sprawled with her hands and feet at odd angles. The woman squealed in fright when someone yanked her up, and then rushed up the stairs.

Again, laugher bubbled from deep in Stuart's gut. The situation was ludicrous. Of all the hardships his family had faced in recent months, if this was the worst fate could do to him, he was one lucky bastard.

He imagined the three women, not that he had any idea what Lila Maclean looked like. The only one that held any appeal was Cait.

"Ye will keep yer word to my daughter."

"It was not I who broke the betrothal, but ye," Stuart rebutted.

"Do not contradict me," the laird replied. "Ye remain

without a wife, therefore ye can marry Flora."

Stuart looked to the other men in the room and then to two maids who stood frozen with trays of food. Obviously, they were unsure if to serve or wait.

One of them gave him a worried look.

Like a maiden, he'd been kidnapped and would be forced to marry.

"Will my virtue also be taken by force?" Stuart asked while staring at the laird. Once again it was hard not to laugh.

A chuckle escaped. "Ye should be aware that I am not a virgin."

The Uisdein, Ethan, and the others exchanged annoyed looks, as he began laughing so hard, he was doubled over.

"Not another word. And stop laughing," Laird Uisdein growled. "Ye must marry Flora."

Stuart could barely speak between each eruption of laughter. "Mar-ry. I… must marry…" He laughed so hard his sides ached and unable to stand, he lowered to the floor. "My predicament is to choose between three women… ha ha ha…"

"What is the matter with him?" the Uisdein asked.

"He was laughing and throwing up on the bìrlinn," Ethan replied. "I have never seen a man in hysterics, but I do believe that is what happens."

"They are here," someone announced, which for some reason made him laugh even harder. It was to the point that he too wondered if he'd gone absolutely mad. Stuart pulled himself up to a chair breathing hard in an effort to regain some semblance of composure.

"Ye either marry or die." The Uisdein warned him and then turned away and shouted, "Where in the devil is Flora?"

"She and yer wife have barricaded themselves in her bedchamber, my laird," someone said.

If not for the fact he was in pain from laughing so hard, Stuart would have erupted into more. Instead, he shook his head and said, "I'm going home." He straightened and stumbled through the great room and out the door.

No one stopped him.

Upon reaching the gates, guards blocked him from leaving and without a weapon he was at their mercy. In that moment, he considered the fact that if he died today, it didn't matter.

He walked up to one of the guards and punched him in the stomach as hard as he could. Caught by surprise, the man doubled over.

When he was grabbed from behind, Stuart swung and with great satisfaction felt his fist sink into someone's face. He fought with all his might, not caring about the consequences. Unfortunately, after laughing so hard, he was weak. It didn't matter. He reached deep into his last resources of strength and managed to hold his own for a few minutes.

Obviously, the guards had been instructed to contain him, not kill him, because they did not draw their swords. Four against one, Stuart was aware he would lose the fight, but it did not stop him from doing as much damage as he could.

When a strike sunk into his gut, he doubled over letting out a loud whoosh of breath. He tried to lift his arms to defend against the next blow, but it was impossible he'd used up his last bit of strength.

Just as he fell to the ground, war cries sounded, and arrows flew overhead impaling the ground all around him.

What was his brother thinking? He could be struck as well.

Then again, fury made little sense.

Realizing his brother would not stop until he got his revenge, Stuart took advantage of the guard's distraction and raced over to the wall and stood next to the gates where the arrows would not strike.

Thundering hooves were quickly followed by the gates hit by battering rams and flying open. The guards had been slow to close them, so the Ross warriors were able to breach moments later.

Darach's blond mane flew around his head as he swung his sword from atop his horse.

Too weak to move after the beating he'd sustained all Stuart could do was watch as the scene unfolded before him.

When Duncan's deep growl sounded, Stuart pitied those coming against the giant.

Caelan jumped down from his horse to fight a group of men. Like a berserker, he left bodies in his wake, not hesitating but instead stepping over them as he attacked one after another. It was almost fascinating to see the otherwise proper Scot turned into a relentless killer.

The sounds of battle filled the air. Men shouting orders. Swords clanging together. The powerful hooves of warhorses striking the ground. All mixed in with the groans of the dying. The unfortunate ones who'd been unable to seek shelter, scurried in terror as there was no mercy from the attackers.

Doing his best to stand, he managed to get to his feet; but moments later, he stumbled backward onto the ground. The fight had taken the last of his strength, all he could do was sit in the grass and watch as his brothers became destroyers.

The Ross warriors breached the house and sometime later,

the Uisdein and his family were dragged out. The sons were badly beaten, the laird, his wife, and Flora looked to be unharmed.

Stuart got to his feet and stumbled forward. Duncan spotted him, jumped from his horse, and hurried to him. "Are ye injured?"

"The damsel in distress will live," Stuart replied bitterly. The bad taste in his mouth growing with each moment.

Darach stalked to where warriors held the Uisdein and his family. "I warned ye I would not take kindly to ye ever provoking me again." His deep voice rumbled over the people gathered that had escaped his wrath.

"Which one?" Darach said motioning to the Uisdein's sons who were forced to their knees. "Choose!" he growled. "Which one dies for ye daring to take my brother."

The Uisdein's eyes rounded in horror. "Stuart made a vow. He was to marry…" He stopped talking seeming to realize the absurdity of his words. Then he took a step forward, reached for the sword in Darach's hand, and lifted it to his own throat.

"Neither of my sons will pay for my deed."

"Very well," Darach said.

"No!" Flora cried out and stood between Darach and her father. "Take me. My brothers and father did this because of me."

Her gaze went to Stuart. "I am sorry. I did not mean for things to get to this point."

"No," Ethan said. "It is I, as eldest, who takes responsibility."

Lady Uisdein pushed her husband forward. "Take responsibility for yer actions. My children should not pay."

There was a beat of silence and seconds later the Uisdein sunk to his knees then fell forward onto the ground. A bright red puddle formed around the Uisdein's head. There was a dagger in his right hand. The man had cut his own throat.

Lady Uisdein screamed and collapsed. Flora took her mother in her arms and they held each other tight, as her two brothers gathered around their dead father.

Darach walked away from the grisly scene. "Let us return home."

THE SEA WAS calm as dozens of Ross bìrlinns traversed the blue expanse back to South Uist and Ross lands. Stuart sat away from the others not sure he could speak. His brothers seemed to sense he needed time and kept their distance. Instead, they discussed the logistics of what had occurred and how it could have been done better.

"Am I a training lesson?" Stuart asked looking at Duncan, who'd been explaining something about the ways the men had formed during the short battle.

"Every battle is an opportunity to learn," Darach replied.

In silence, he looked over the water to another bìrlinn, which Caelan was on. It seemed Darach had left the helm of the lairdship in Ewan's able hands.

"I am glad to serve some purpose." Bitterness dripped from each word.

His brothers exchanged a look, which he recognized as them thinking he needed time to get over whatever had happened to him.

"I should be overcome and taken away more often. That could be my value."

Darach's jaw tightened, the muscle on the side of his face flexing. "What ye are is an idiot."

"True," Stuart said. "I am the idiot that needs rescuing, while the rest of ye . . . ye are the true warriors. Each of ye."

He motioned to Duncan. "Ye were stolen away, Father abandoned ye to be sold. Ye survived years of captivity and ye remain a good man and became a great warrior."

He could not stop now. "Ewan… well should we even discuss what Father did to him? He too was gone for years because of the evil one that gave us life. And ye," he said to Darach. "Father killed yer mother. And ye were charged with taking over the lairdship from a man who was hated by the people."

"What does this have to do with anything?" Darach replied. "None of us can help our lot in life."

"That is just it. I have no lot. I have been afforded a good life. Because of the sufferings of my brothers, I gained richness and stability. Why did ye risk so much to come for me?"

His brothers were silent. It must have been because what he said was true.

"Ye are our brother, we would give our lives for ye, just as we know ye would do for us." Duncan glared at him. "Stop being an idiot."

Stuart suddenly felt hollow, the sensation so horrifying he wanted to scream. Instead, he met Darach's gaze. "I must go. I cannot remain at the keep. Allow me to go."

"Where?" his brothers asked in unison.

"Ye should consider this more," Darach said. "Aye, ye have

benefitted, but ye have also fought side by side when it was needed. Ye are not without some of the sufferings we endured at the hands of our father."

"Ye must allow me to go," Stuart repeated too exhausted to argue further.

# CHAPTER EIGHT

DESPITE HER BANDAGED hand, Cait did what she could to help care for the injured men who'd been attacked in the forest. All four guardsmen had been knocked unconscious and a couple of them had nasty cuts to their heads. Artair Ross had received a deep wound to his side, but still managed to ride back and alert them of the attack. He was recovering in one of the bedchambers.

Cots were being set up in the great hall for any injured men returning from Benbecula.

Lady Isobel came to stand next to Cait, who was awkwardly washing an injured man's face with her left hand. She looked up expecting the woman to say something.

"I'm sure they'll be returning soon." She looked to the doorway; worry etched on her pretty face. "I am glad Darach took a large contingency."

"Everyone will return safely," Cait said praying Stuart was unharmed.

"Ye should rest," Isobel said. "We may be up all night once the men return."

"I am not tired," Cait replied. "Surprisingly, my hand does not hurt much."

"Come sit with me for a moment." Isobel took her by the arm. "There is something we must discuss."

Curious, Cait followed her to a bench at the long dining tables nearby. "Is something wrong?"

"No, not necessarily." Isobel seemed to struggle to formulate what she wanted to say. "It is just that we find it awkward for ye to remain in the servant's quarters, given the situation."

"What situation?" Cait asked genuinely confused.

Isobel gave her a wan smile. "Ye should know this. I may be wrong in sharing, but my husband told me that Stuart plans to court ye."

Her eyes widened and she let out a long breath. "Me? I am a servant."

"Aye. I suppose love and attraction do not take note of such things. Ewan's wife, Catriona, was a servant. Darach's cousin, Malcolm Ross—who is also a laird—married Elsbeth, a humble healer who lived at a nearby village."

Mind racing over what to say, Cait swallowed. "I am not sure what to think. I do not think my laird heard him correctly."

Isobel smiled. "When he returns and asks to speak to ye, at least now ye know what to expect."

Thankfully, someone called Lady Isobel away before there could be any further discussion about her moving from the servant's quarters.

Cait remained sitting, her mind awhirl. Yes, she'd shared a kiss with Stuart; but surely it had not been enough for him to go to such lengths as declaring to his family that he wished to court her. It was probably to do with her having declared that she would not be a mistress. Perhaps he felt forced to make a declaration after someone spotted them kissing.

Could it be that her half brother had something to do with

it? She would get to the bottom of it. And hopefully avoid Stuart until she was able to figure out why Lady Isobel and the laird expected Stuart to court her.

"They return," Cora called out racing past her toward the kitchen entrance. "I pray Torac was not harmed."

"I am sure he was not," Cait said with more assuredness than she felt. Her brother was an able fighter and although not knowing him long, she'd grown to care for him. "He is well, ye will see." Cait stood smoothed her apron and followed Cora out.

Both Cora and Cait stood in the courtyard and lifted to their toes as mounted warriors came through the gates. First were the head guardsmen—which included Torac—followed by two wagons on which injured had been brought. From what Cait could tell there were not many, but enough to keep them very busy.

Torac dismounted and called out orders. Duncan and Gideon also dismounted and began directing warriors and guards.

A group of lads raced to the well with buckets as Greer instructed them to bring the water into the great hall.

Cait looked to Cora. "Are ye to go speak to my brother?"

"There is no time. We must see about the injured."

It was then she noted that Stuart was helped from the back of a wagon. He hobbled between two warriors that half carried him into the house. His face was swollen, and his tunic shredded and bloody.

"Come, there is much to see about," Greer who'd come out and stood behind them said. "Cora, ye and Finella help the healer. Cait, ye and I will see about feeding the warriors outside."

They hurried back to the kitchen. Although Cait was anxious to know how Stuart fared, in a way she was glad not to be given a different task.

Despite being able to use only her left hand, Cait still managed to do limited work. Women from the village arrived in time to help with the cooking and serving, leaving Cait and Greer to see about refilling cups and ensuring everyone had enough to eat.

They would continue working in shifts through the night.

"I do not know why I am so exhausted," Cait said walking into the kitchen. "I am used to doing more after walking from my home. Last night I was here."

Greer nodded. "Caring for the injured, while worrying about dear ones being hurt is tiring. I am glad that no one was hurt badly."

"How is…How is Mister Stuart? I saw him being helped inside," Cait asked.

The older woman sighed. "He went to his bedchamber and refused to see anyone. Lady Mariel just went up to see about him."

One of the kitchen maids neared, she looked over her shoulder and then whispered, "I hear the Uisdein slit his own throat in front of him. Mister Stuart's betrothed, Flora, was there."

"Betrothed?" Cait blurted.

"Aye," Greer said waving a hand dismissively. "He was once betrothed to Flora Uisdein, but the betrothal was broken by her father. Then after they held our laird captive, the alliance with them was completely severed."

Cait closed her eyes. The day had become more and more bizarre. First, Isobel tells her Stuart is interested in courting her and now, she finds out he had a betrothed. Whatever could happen next?

Her mother had always told Cait not to tempt faith by asking "what next?" She shivered at the realization and prayed not to get any kind of horrible response.

Cait remained in the kitchen wondering what she should do. If only she could seek guidance from her mother. However, there was no possible way she could walk all the way home since she would be needed early to help with the injured and the cooking.

"I do not think I can continue on. I am going to lay down for a few moments," Cait said. After a nod from Greer, she left the kitchen and walked slowly down the corridor toward the servant's quarters.

Lady Mariel appeared; her face drawn. "Ah, there ye are. My goodness, ye look exhausted. I hate to ask this of ye, but I require yer assistance."

Without waiting for a response, she took Cait by the wrist and tugged her past the great room, up the stairs, and into a bedchamber.

Stuart was there on the bed. He looked to either be asleep or unconscious.

"What happened to him?" Cait whispered.

With a dismissive wave, Lady Mariel glowered toward the bed. "Cuts, bumps, bruises. He has a rather nasty cut on his left side, just under his ribs."

"I am afraid I may be too tired to be of much help. I can sit here with him if ye wish," Cait told her, praying the woman would tell her to leave and return later.

The woman neared the bed and pushed at Stuart's shoulder. He mumbled something akin to go away, but it was hard to tell.

"The healer's potion must have been stronger than I thought," Lady Mariel said frowning down at her son.

"I suppose ye can speak to him later."

"About what?"

There was a rapid knock at the door, followed by the laird appearing. He looked to the bed and then to her and his mother. "How is he faring?"

"He is asleep," Lady Mariel said. "I suppose it means he is well. I brought Cait so she could talk to him. Perhaps convince him against the nonsense he was going on about."

"That is not our concern. I do agree they should discuss it in private, but it must be on their terms," Darach Ross said and gave Cait an apologetic look. "Mother, let us leave them be for a while."

The pair left, leaving her standing in the middle of Stuart's bedchamber without any idea what she was supposed to do. What was it she and Stuart had to discuss?

"This is ridiculous," she said nearing the bed and looking down at the slumbering man. He was without a tunic, the bedcovers up across his chest. She poked at his shoulder with one finger, and he barely moved.

"What do they wish us to talk about? I know ye are betrothed—or were. And for whatever reason, yer family thinks ye plan to court me. Ye must wake and set things right."

His eyes flew open, and he met hers for a long moment. "Ye are so very beautiful."

Unsure if he was in his right mind, Cait nodded. "Thank ye. What is it we are to speak about?"

When his eyes fluttered shut, she waited. Then he let out a long sigh. "I want to be with ye Cait. To get to know ye better. Do ye wish the same?" His gaze held questions as he gave her a questioning look. "I do not have much to offer."

Despite the situation, Cait chuckled. "Ye are the laird's brother. How can ye say that? Once ye are recovered perhaps we can finish this discussion."

He nodded. "I am not sure what to do."

"Ye should listen to yer heart. I think ye are an amazing man Mister Stuart."

"Do not call me that. Call me Stuart, Cait." It was as if he could not keep his eyes open. "My Cait."

His head lolled to the side as he fell asleep. Cait wondered if he would remember the conversation. Probably not.

Reaching out with trembling fingers, she touched the side of his face. His skin was cool to the touch. "I wish I could believe what ye said."

She eyed an oversized chair that had a blanket thrown over one arm. It was too alluring to pass up. No one, except for the laird and his mother, knew where she was. If she took a short nap, no one would be the wiser.

Her lips curved as she curled up on the soft cushion, pulled the cover over herself, and promptly fell into a deep slumber.

WHEN SHE WOKE, Cait realized how deeply she slept because not only was it dark outside, but Caelan sat in a chair close to the bed speaking to Stuart in low tones.

Cait had to press her lips together not to gasp. Could it be neither of them knew she was there? No. They knew. Hence the whispering.

Cait closed her eyes tightly, pretending to continue sleeping.

"I think ye should decide what it is ye wish to do," Caelan said. "If ye feel as if it is time for a change, do not allow anyone or anything to stop ye."

It sounded as if Stuart wanted to do something but was being held back. Cait wished with all her might not to hear any more of the conversation that was not meant for her ears.

"Lennox Maclean is sending his sister here. She wishes to learn about ledgers and such. It will be ye that spends time teaching her," Stuart said. "I do not wish to meet the lass and do something that can ruin relations with the new laird."

Caelan murmured a reply that Cait could not make out. She waited a few beats and pretended to wake by yawning loudly and stretching. She slid clumsily to her feet. "I apologize for falling asleep. I was to look after ye." She gave them a quick glance. "I will see about something for ye to eat."

"I am not hungry…"

She hurried from the room before Stuart finished the sentence.

The great hall was quiet, most of the injured were asleep. Thankfully the only ones about were the healer and his assistant.

Cait walked past them and headed to the servant's quarters. Once inside the safety of the tiny room, she melted into the only chair and bowed her head.

From what she overheard, it had sounded as if someone was coming to visit, and they would bring a woman who

Stuart was supposed to meet.

All that had happened between her and Stuart was a simple kiss. In her limited knowledge of men, Stuart had not come close to declaring himself. He was kind. And might possibly be attracted to her. Nothing more.

Cait lifted her head, unsure what to do with the rest of the day. What she needed to do was go home and spend time with her mother.

Lady Ross had told her to take time off from her duties and she would do just that.

# CHAPTER NINE

IT HAD BEEN a night filled with tossing and turning. Stuart's mind going from one thing to the other and still he had no idea what he wished to do. Searching deep inside himself, he came up empty.

Nothing motivated him and that was the problem. It infuriated him that for so long he'd lived in the shadows of his brothers. He'd always done what he could to help but had lost a sense of who he truly was.

Although a restlessness had come over him, the stirring in his soul came without direction or guide. Instead, all he felt was a deep sense of wanting to do something different. To find his true purpose.

Then there was Cait. Despite how hard he tried to put any thoughts of her aside, the beautiful woman invaded his every waking moment. The thought of not including her—in whatever his future may be—brought hesitation. He'd dreamt of having a conversation with her and asking if she wanted to be with him. Because he wasn't sure he could leave her behind.

She would not remain unmarried for long and the thought of her with someone else was unbearable.

It was a wonder she wasn't being pursued already. Then again, perhaps she was, suitors weren't always obvious.

With a growl, he threw the blankets aside, and pushing

past the pain from the beating he'd received, he got up. There was much to do, and he could not remain abed waiting for inspiration to come.

One thing he knew for certain: His destiny's call was strong.

Stuart stomped down the stairs to the great hall. There were a few cots with injured men along a far wall in front of the large hearth. The fire from it would keep them warm as they recovered from their injuries.

Several servants meandered between the beds, reassuring the men as they replaced the wet rags on their foreheads.

He continued to the study, where he walked in to find Darach and Isobel in a passionate embrace. The couple was so engrossed in each other, they didn't hear him enter and only pulled apart when he dragged a chair back and sat.

Isobel blushed and smiled up at her husband before looking to Stuart. "I am glad to see ye about. How do ye feel?"

"Why are ye not in bed?" Darach asked, his overprotectiveness rearing as he assessed Stuart's injuries.

"I am not so injured that there was need for me to stay in bed any longer."

After a lingering look to her husband—that promised more to come—Isobel walked out. Darach followed her progress for a bit before turning his attention to Stuart.

"Ye asked for me to let ye go. What do ye mean to do? Where do ye intend to go?"

The direct questions caught Stuart off guard. He'd expected Darach to try to talk him out of leaving.

He was prepared to let his brother know he still planned to leave, without a destination or a purpose in mind. Now he wondered if it would sound childish and petty to leave when he was needed at the keep.

"I can go to one of the posts, either in the north or south. We've had two encroachments in the last few months, we need more vigilance."

His brother watched him for a few moments. "Every man needs to prove their worth. Ye have proven to be brave and taken charge when it was needed. There is no reason to go away. I need ye here."

There was a sinking feeling in the pit of his stomach as he tried to explain to his brother that his life had been quite the opposite. He'd not done anything as worthwhile as any of his brothers, except for Gideon, who was too young yet to compare himself with.

"I have done nothing more than any other guard. Stood up for our clan and protected the family." Standing, he stalked across the room. "I want to do something that matters. To our clan. To ye. To myself."

"Very well," Darach said moving closer. "Perhaps I am selfish in wanting our family to remain close. I understand the need to have yer own life."

"I am restless and have to do something."

"Go to yer land. The people in the village there are in great need."

For a moment he was confused. His lands were a day's ride to the northwest. He'd not had time to return since the first time he'd gone there several months earlier. For whatever reason, his father had ignored that region for years and the people were accustomed to it. If anything, they were probably the ones who needed leadership the least.

"They are independent and will be resistant to anyone coming to bring them under any control."

"They are Clan Ross and must be loyal to me and our family. I have had reports they are going through a trying time. Apparently, the constable is overstepping in his authority. They need ye, Stuart."

He let out a long breath. "So, I have failed them as well."

"If anyone failed them it was me. So much has happened that I've barely had time to take care of those who need us. I have kept ye away from them for too long. Do as I say and stop making it about ye."

The words sunk in, and Stuart straightened. "Ye are right."

"Be sure to take enough seed, livestock, and whatever ye think is needed to settle there. Ye have a lot of work to do to prepare. I suggest ye get started."

For the first time in a long time, Stuart was filled with anticipation of what was to come. "I will ask to see who wishes to go with me. I can find farmers and men from the village once I'm there to help with all that is required, but first, I will need to have people alongside me that I can trust. Can I take six men with me?"

"Take as many as ye think are required. Give them the option of remaining or returning if they do not like it."

Darach pulled the map of Ross lands and spread it across the desk in front of them. He then circled the lands Stuart was gifted upon becoming laird. "There is a loch and ye have the seashore not too far. Ensure the people are utilizing both for their needs."

"Here." He pointed to a specific spot. "There is a house here that with some repairs will be a good place for ye to live.

There is another one in town."

Stuart nodded his chest expanding at the thought that this had to be his purpose. "Thank ye, brother."

"Ye may be cursing me after a few weeks of trying to bring those people and the land to heel." Darach chuckled.

Walking out of the study, Stuart asked a servant about his mother and was told she and Isobel were in the parlor. He found the women sewing in quiet companionship.

"Mother," he stated, getting her attention. "I just spoke to Darach. I have decided to go and live on my lands."

His mother's lips curved, but her gaze was sad. "I do not wish for ye to leave. Why do ye feel the need to?"

"I am needed there more than here. My lands and people are not faring well."

"Do ye wish for Cait and I to go with ye?"

At the mention of the maid's name, his stomach tumbled. "The house is not habitable yet. Ye can come once I settle, and all is as it should be."

"Are ye to marry then, before leaving?" Isobel asked. "Lila Maclean is set to arrive soon, and we should have a good reason for turning her away."

Stuart blew out a breath. "At this time, I do not wish to marry the maid or anyone else for that matter. I have much to do. I care little what Lila Maclean, or her brother are told."

At Isobel's wide gaze locked to a place past him, Stuart turned to see Cait standing in the doorway with a tray, looking pale as a ghost.

Somehow, she managed to hold her head high as she walked in. The tray shook just enough to alert those in the room that she was doing her best to keep her emotions under control.

Everyone was silent, except his mother. “Thank ye, Cait. How is yer hand? Ye should be resting.”

“I am well enough to do my tasks,” Cait said. “I prefer to work and take care of my family rather than expect anyone else to do so. I will be going home for a pair of days. Greer has allowed it.”

Isobel nodded. “Aye, of course. Take as long as ye need.”

Head bowed, she brushed past him and left.

His mother stood. “Ye are an idiot.” She walked out behind Cait leaving only him and a glaring Isobel.

“Why did ye say that?” Isobel demanded. “Ye have made us all believe ye are interested in Cait. I cannot believe ye were so cruel.”

“Do not walk out.” Stuart moved sideways to block Isobel from leaving.

“I am walking out. I have nothing to say to ye.”

He shook his head. “I do care for Cait. If I were to remain here, there’s a definite chance I would court her.”

“Ugh.” Isobel took a couple of steps but stopped when Stuart blocked her once again.

“Can ye explain it to her?” he asked. “I need to do this. To take care of the people I am responsible for.”

The woman lifted her hands up. “Oh, no. I definitely will not. Ye hurt her and it is up to ye to explain yer quest for manly greatness and hope she forgives ye.”

When he looked down, Isobel dashed around him and left.

A few moments later, he trudged back through the great room to the kitchen. Greer and her group of cooks and maids hurried about working on meal preparation. The red-faced woman glanced up and looked at him with concern.

"How are ye faring?" She placed a warm hand to his forearm. "If ye go to the dining room, I will have someone bring ye something."

Stuart shook his head. "I do not require anything. I seek Cait."

Finella, Greer's daughter, waved to the window. "She left in a cart. I believe she went home to rest."

Leaving the kitchen, he headed outside to where the guards trained. Several stood in circles talking, others practiced. He spotted Gideon and a guard sparing while Artair sat on a stool and watched.

"I must speak to ye," he said to his brother as he walked up. Though he made sure to keep enough distance to not get accidentally cut.

"About what?" Gideon called out and blocked a strike.

"He is trying to help ye, by distracting ye," Artair called out laughing when Gideon jumped back and yelled out a curse.

Both men lowered their swords and waited for him to approach. "What is it?" Gideon asked wiping sweat from his face with the front of his tunic. "I am not in the mood to discuss duties. I am preparing to go to the south post. Or is it the north?" He looked up to the sky as if for an answer. "I forget."

"South," Artair said in a bored tone.

Stuart met their gazes. "I have decided to live on my lands and see about the people there. What I want to ask is who ye think would wish to go with me."

The duo gaped at him as if not understanding.

"Is this permanent?" Gideon asked, his eyes widening.

"Why now?

Artair studied him with confusion. "Where are yer lands?

"Northwest coast," he said to Artair, before answering Gideon. "Aye, it is permanent."

His brother and cousin exchanged looks. "Why?" Gideon repeated.

"Because I have to see about the people. They are in need and it is my duty to see to them."

"I will go with ye," Artair said without hesitation. "Ye cannot go alone."

"What about yer father?" Stuart asked. "Is he still unwell?"

Artair frowned in thought. "I will speak to him; he is doing better.

"I plan to take some men with me. I can find servants and someone to farm the land from those that live there," Stuart informed them.

Gideon frowned. "I could go with ye. My lands are almost empty and do not require much."

"There are two fishing villages on yer lands," Stuart replied. "When the time is right, ye need to start visiting more often."

His brother shrugged. "I go every fortnight or so. The people there are self-reliant and they often come here to speak to Darach. No need for me to do much."

Once again, Stuart considered how he'd been too involved in his duties, not to notice his own responsibilities. He had not been aware that Gideon went to his lands so often to see about the people.

"Ye cannot go," he told Artair. "Uncle Angus is not well and requires yer help."

"Then who goes with ye?" Gideon asked.

"I was thinking I might ask Ewan to go with me and help me set up. He recently built a home and settled into his lands. Already he has productive fields and is self-sufficient with livestock and such."

Gideon nodded. "Grand idea."

Mind made up, he discussed a few more things with Gideon and Artair before heading out to visit Ewan.

He would have to see about Cait before leaving. But first, he had to start getting things in order.

DESPITE SOME SORENESS, the ride to Ewan's lands gave him a chance to clear his head. More than anything Cait was at the forefront of his mind. The look on her face when she'd overheard what he'd said in the parlor made him cringe.

He'd hurt her feelings and it wasn't fair. She shouldn't have to pay for his confusion about what he wanted. A part of him wanted her to be in his life so badly that he almost turned the horse toward the cottage to find her and convince her to go with him. But no matter how much he wanted to, it made no sense to approach her about leaving. Not only did he not have a clear plan, but they'd not had enough time to get to know one another.

BY THE TIME he arrived at Ewan's, Stuart was excited at the prospect of starting the new phase of his life. Spotting his brother standing by the corrals that housed several horses, he dismounted and walked over.

Everyone said he and Ewan could be twins. His brother had the same dark wavy hair that fell to his shoulders. They stood at the same height. And they were both archers, to boot.

He approached Ewan and they embraced.

"What brings ye?" his brother asked looking him over. Upon noticing the bruising on his face, he frowned. "I could have come to the keep."

"I am not so hurt that it bothered me to ride here. I came to speak to ye about the process of settling here on yer lands. Darach suggested—and I agree—that it is time for me to go to my lands and see about the people. It is time to take control of my life."

His brother met his gaze for a long moment. "I understand. But remember ye always have us to help and assist ye as needed."

"I have no doubt that ye and our brothers will be more than happy to meddle even without my asking."

Ewan chuckled nodding. "Very true."

"Which is why I want to ask if ye will go with me and look it over? I need yer advice."

Ewan's expression was warm, it made Stuart realize how lucky he was that despite, or perhaps because of their father's cruel ways, he and his brothers were so close. They'd depended on one another since childhood and that had forged a strong bond.

His brother opened his arms and turned in a circle. "This is hard work and at times ye will feel like giving up, but in the end it is worth it." He met Stuart's gaze. "Now, I cannot think of anything better than having my own home, productive lands, and a beautiful wife to share it with."

FOR DAYS, STUART worked tirelessly to prepare for his upcoming move. It was easier than he expected to find men who wished to travel. Dougal Ross—a third cousin—and his wife, Bree, were eager to accompany him. Also, a group of single men volunteered even after he told them it would be hard work. It seemed some loved adventure and their excitement was contagious.

Anton was a harder sell. Although the young man wished to go, he wasn't sure about living away from his family.

"I have made a decision." Anton approached him early one day.

"Oh?" Stuart said as Anton stood beside the hearth in his bedchamber. Despite Stuart usually not requiring his services, Anton took his duties as squire seriously. Every morning he appeared at Stuart's door with news about the weather outside, or to let him know how his horse was doing.

"Father insists I go, so I will." Anton gave him a crooked smile that did not disguise his nervousness.

"It is a long ride to the village from there, but ye can make it in a day. No need to worry. If ye wish to visit yer family, I will allow it."

Anton brightened. "That is what Father said."

Stuart found himself anxious to get going. But first there was livestock to choose from his brother's herds, and decisions as to what needed to be taken. Already there were wagons overflowing with grain, seeds, plantings, and tools.

The ones who were going also had their own belongings to pack onto wagons. Albeit the single men didn't plan to bring much.

It had been several days since he'd seen Cait. Once she

returned from her time away, it was obvious she did everything in her power to avoid him. He'd even tried to seek her out in the kitchen and then in the garden, but she must have seen him coming and hid.

At first meal, the family sat in the dining room, away from those who came early and mingled in the great hall.

"I suggest ye leave behind anything of sentimental value in yer bedchamber," his mother advised once he sat. "Ye do not wish items to become lost while ye work."

Isobel frowned in his direction. "Who is going with ye? I hear Bree and her husband are. I will miss our trips to the village."

"Aye, Dougal and Bree are going. So are four guardsmen, Anton and two men from the village."

The rest of the conversation as they ate was about his upcoming trip and the more they talked, the more anxious he was to head out.

When he finished eating, he hurried up to his bedchamber to begin packing. A cool breeze blew in through the open window and he went to peer out. Cait was standing at the well with Cora, who was quite animated and pointing towards where the guards sparred. Cait shook her head and crossed her arms.

From where he was, he couldn't see Cait's expression clearly, but from the way she stood she was not happy about whatever the other woman had said.

Cait took Cora's arm and they walked around the side of the house. Intrigued, Stuart went to his other window to see what happened.

The women stood watching the guards practicing. Every so

often they'd talk and then continue watching.

Stuart looked to the field to see who was there. It could be Cora was telling Cait about someone who was interested in courting her. And although reluctant, Cait had agreed to speak to whomever it was.

Upon noting they had an audience, several of the men picked up the pace, grunting loudly to get Cait and Cora's attention.

It was ridiculous to be annoyed and yet, Stuart found himself storming from the room, down the stairs, through the great room, and out the front door.

When he rounded the house, Cait and Cora were still speaking in low tones.

"Speak to him. Perhaps he will tell ye what..." Cora stopped talking. "Mister Stuart."

Cait didn't turn around. "Mister Stuart," she said turning her face just a bit so not to be disrespectful.

"May I speak to ye, Cait?" Stuart asked looking to Cora, who remained where she was her gaze pinned on Cait. Finally, she gave Cait a worried look and walked away.

Since Cait didn't turn to face him, Stuart rounded her standing between her and the guard's field. "I have been meaning to speak to ye. I owe ye an apology."

"There is no need to apologize for a comment I was not supposed to hear." Her reply was curt. Her gaze remained fixed on a point past his right shoulder. "If that is all Mister Stuart, I have duties to attend to."

"It was thoughtless of me to refer to ye in such a manner. Ye are important to me and I am not sure why I said it. The only excuse I have is that I am a horse's arse."

She didn't move or look up at him. "I am a servant; therefore, ye did not say anything that should affect me."

"It was thoughtless and not at all true. I do have feelings for ye and hope to get to know ye better."

They were silent for a long moment until Cait finally sighed. "May I go now please?"

"Forgive me," he repeated. "Allow me to make it up to ye."

She nodded. "Ye have nothing to make up for."

"I am leaving," Stuart blurted. "To my lands."

"Aye, I have heard. I wish ye well." Again, her tone was flat.

As she went to turn away, he reached out and touched her still crossed arm. "Perhaps ye and yer family will wish to move there. Once I get everything settled."

It was then that her gaze lifted to his. For a moment he was struck silent by her beauty. The woman appealed to him like no other. Leaving her there would be one of the hardest things he could ever do.

"Say ye will come," Stuart repeated.

"I cannot." She let out a long breath. "I do not understand what ye wish from me. I have been clear that I will not be more than a servant to this household."

"Is something wrong?" Torac, her half brother neared, his eyes fixed on Stuart. "Mister Stuart is there something ye require of Cait?"

Stuart shook his head. He was not intimidated by Torac—quite the opposite—he admired the willingness of the man to stand up for his sister. "I was telling Cait that I am leaving and asked if she, her mother, and her brother would be interested in going to the northwest eventually."

Torac studied him for a long moment before looking to Cait. "It could be something beneficial for ye. To start at a new household."

"I will consider it," Cait said, and gave her brother a searching look before turning to him. "Is that all Mister Stuart?"

"Will ye truly think about it?"

She let out a sigh. "I will."

Stuart nodded.

She then looked at her brother. "I must speak to ye about something that is of great concern."

Dismissed, Stuart walked away, lighter at the being given a glimmer of hope that Cait would consider moving.

# CHAPTER TEN

CAIT GLARED AT her brother. "Cora is bereft. Why do ye ignore her?"

"I have been busy. Ye know with that little thing called: a battle. And I have been given new responsibilities as head guard for a contingent of men."

Rolling her eyes, Cait gave him a pointed look. "Ye returned unscathed. Thank God. Honestly, I am glad. But Torac ye cannot simply ignore Cora after… well after everything."

At least her intimidating brother managed to look uncomfortable at her words. His wide shoulders lifted and lowered as he considered what to say.

"I need time. She wishes for more than I am willing to give now."

"Then ye should not have taken things so far. Her heart is broken, and she's scared. Her parents wish her to marry someone from the village."

Torac wiped away the sweat from his face with his forearm. "It would not be a bad thing for her to marry someone who will give her all she wants."

"Torac," Cait gasped his name. "Ye will have her marry someone else and not bat an eye?"

Her brother's temper came to the surface. "Let it be Cait. This is none of yer concern. What about ye and Stuart Ross.

Why does he show so much interest in ye?"

He was not about to abruptly changed the subject and throw her off balance. "He caused me to cut my hand. Before that, he happened to run into me in the forest just as I was hiding from a boar. There is nothing else. I believe Lady Ross is behind it. Making him feel responsible for my well-being. Nothing more."

Torac gave her a dubious look, then glanced over his shoulder toward the front door. "Never forget dear sister, people like them are not like us. They marry within their social circle and any interest in us is for nothing more than a dalliance."

"That is the reason I am not certain about going to the northwest. I do not wish for him to think I aspire to be more than a servant."

"I believe Stuart Ross to be an honorable man. If he brings ye there, he will give ye a good position. Perhaps head cook or housekeeper," Torac admitted. "But just make sure he is aware ye will not be interested in anything more."

Cait let out a long breath. "A post that would allow me to provide more for Mother, would be good. I will think on it."

Watching her brother walk away, she considered how she'd feel when Stuart married a woman of his status. If she went with him, would it be possible for her to push her feelings away? It was not an easy choice. On the one hand, if she went with him, it would be easier to support her family. On the other, every day she'd be forced to watch Stuart with his wife.

"What did he say?" Cora asked as soon as Cait walked into the kitchen. The kitchen maids were chopping vegetables for last meal, not paying them any mind. Still, Cait did not wish to be overheard.

"Come let us take cups out to the great hall and begin setting up."

Seeming to understand, Cora began placing cups on the tray, in clumsy stacks. Cait did the same only much neater. Keeping her tray light so that she could hold it using both hands.

They hurried to the great room, which—lucky for them—was empty.

"He does not care for me, does he?" Cora said, her eyes bright with tears. "Just say it Cait."

She wanted to come up with a way to convey the truth without making Cora feel horrible. And yet, Cait considered if it were her, she'd want the pure unadulterated truth.

"He claims not to feel ready for any type of relationship. I do not know what made him change his feelings. Perhaps it was going to battle."

"Does he need time?" Cora asked looking hopeful. "Should I be patient?"

"Nay, Cora. Ye should not wait for him."

Cora's face fell and she collapsed into a heap on the floor. Thankfully, she managed to keep the tray from spilling all the contents. Ever so slowly Cait took the tray and placed it on a nearby table. "I am so very sorry."

"I may just need to get away from here and not have to see him every day." Cora covered her face with both hands.

"I am so sorry. He should be more responsible with his actions toward ye," Cait replied and hugged her friend.

Cait wondered why a person's heart led one to feel for

someone who did not return the sentiment. She ached for Cora. Perhaps this was a lesson for her as well. How ridiculous that her ignorant heart cared little about status.

"I will ask Mister Stuart to go with him," Cora announced. "I am sure he will require help from someone who is familiar with the way things are done."

Cait's stomach dipped. "I would miss ye terribly."

"Then ye should come as well…" Cora stopped. "I am sorry, ye are in the same predicament as I. What did Mister Stuart wish to tell ye?"

Cait looked around to ensure not to be overheard. "To apologize for saying the hurtful remark in the parlor. He seemed sincere."

They gathered their trays to continue about their tasks in the great hall just as Lady Isobel and Lady Mariel walked in. It was obvious they weren't sure how to address Cait, so she bobbed her head and dipped just a bit in a curtsy. "Good day, Lady Isobel. Lady Mariel."

"How is yer hand?" Lady Isobel asked.

"It is healing well, thank ye." Cait hurried to the farthest table to go about setting it, praying neither woman would follow her. It was painful enough to have been embarrassed in front of them, but now the awkwardness remained. Over time it would fade, and she would return to being just another servant in the household.

Darach, Gideon, and Stuart entered and continued toward the high board. Cait tried to figure out a way to return to the kitchen without attracting their attention.

"I'll have ale," the laird called out. Cait looked up noting that he spoke to a kitchen maid who'd followed them with a pitcher in each hand.

While they were served, she picked up the now empty tray and hurried from the room.

"IT IS A wonderful proposition," her mother said. They'd just finished eating and sat in chairs outside the front door of the cottage enjoying the last of the daylight. "If we go with Mister Stuart, ye will have a good position and yer brother will have work as well."

Her mother studied her for a moment. "Ye must push those feelings aside lass. Men like him, while enticing, are not meant for the likes of women like us."

"I understand Mother. I heard it from Torac as well," Cait replied. "That is why I hesitate to accept. I do not wish to continue pining over him. It is ridiculous. 'Tis not like I am a wee lass with little sense."

Her mother laughed. "When it comes to matters of the heart, we are always wee lasses."

"Accept the offer dear," her mother said. "When he sends for ye, we will be ready to go."

A rabbit hopped past and Cait considered trapping it until she noticed two tiny ones following behind it. Her lips curved as the rabbit hurried her brood back under the bushes.

"We have traveled far to settle here," she said absently. "Lady Ross assures me I will always have a position. If we do not go, ye do not have to worry Mother."

At her mother's silence, she looked to her and noted she'd fallen asleep. Although she'd grown stronger, she was still delicate. Cait did want a better, more comfortable life for her mother. A home without drafts or a leaky roof.

She let out a sigh. "I could accept the offer."

"Good," her mother replied, her lips curving and eyes remaining closed.

Cait laughed. "Mother, ye were faking!"

THE NEXT DAY, Cait took her time walking back to the keep as she didn't have to work until the next day. It was just easier to leave the day before her shift began to keep from having to walk there so early in the morning.

A long sigh escaped at the thought of Stuart leaving soon. As much as she had tried to fight against it, she was deeply fond of him. Accepting his offer to go to the new house still meant she would not see him for a long while. According to what she'd heard, it would be months before the house on his land was habitable.

So, she had to wait. Her mother would not withstand living in a temporary shelter, exposed to the elements. Although it was early fall, it rained often and there was no guarantee all would be completed before winter when the weather would become decidedly colder.

The sound of a horse's nicker brought her out of her musings. She stepped sideways from the path to avoid being seen. Then peering around the tree, she saw Stuart. He held up a pair of ducks. "For yer mother."

He beamed with pride and she couldn't help but smile. "She will be delighted. Thank ye."

"I will take them to her now."

When he rode around her and went in the direction of the cottage, Cait wasn't sure if she should follow. Instead, she decided to continue toward the keep.

It wasn't much later when he returned and reported that indeed her mother was quite happy with the offering. He dismounted and walked alongside her.

"I have been thinking," he started. "That I did not properly make ye an offer to come with me."

Cait held out a hand to stop him from speaking. She wanted to accept, but first she had to find out as much as she could, as this move would not be only for her, but her family as well.

"Tell me about yer lands."

He nodded. "It is not as flat as here. There are tall hills and a deep valley. Near the hill furthest from the seashore is where the larger house sits. The nearby village is by the shoreline and a bit smaller than the one near here, my family has a smaller house there. The people there are a hardy lot. A bit rough, but I suppose that is the way of living by the sea."

"Where will ye live?"

"At the larger house, which is in dire need of repairs."

He became animated as he spoke. "I wish to clear the land and raise livestock and have fields of wheat and . . . well, lots of other crops. To be honest, I am leaving that portion to men who understand farming."

"It will take ye a long time to have everything repaired and ready then?"

"Aye," he met her gaze. "It will take months." Stuart took her hand, and she was too shocked by the action to do more than allow it. "Come let us sit for a moment."

They walked off the path and into a small clearing. Like most highlanders, he had a tartan in the bag that hung from the saddle. He spread it on the ground and motioned for Cait to sit. Then he produced a carrot and gave it to his horse. Finally, he pulled a wineskin from the same bag and sat down next to her.

"I understand yer reasons for hesitating. It is all my fault. To help ye understand, I must explain that compared to my brothers, I have felt adrift. It is as if each of them has accomplished something. This move, to take control of what is mine and rebuild it, has given me purpose. I wish to share my life there with ye."

Cait met his gaze. There was so much in his eyes that she didn't understand. It was as if he wanted her as a woman, but at the same time, she sensed he held back.

"I do not know what to say…"

"Say that ye will consider it."

She smiled and nodded. "I am considering it but understand that I have to think of my mother and brother first."

"Of course. They are welcome to come as well. It may be late fall, perhaps winter, before the house will be habitable."

A noisy flock of birds flew overhead, and they both looked up following their flight. Cait wished time would stand still and that for a while longer, she could pretend Stuart was a man who could be hers. Someone she could trust with everything. Her heart. Her body. Her soul.

"What are ye thinking about?" he asked.

"What I have noticed about ye," Cait replied. "Each of yer brothers look to ye for council. They trust ye to keep a level head and see predicaments from all angles. Even the villagers and servants, when presented with a particularly difficult situation ask to speak to ye." She let out a breath. "Ye have been fulfilling a very important role in the family all along."

His eyes widened and he studied her before finally nodding slowly. "Thank ye for saying that. It was not something I had considered."

"I am right in what I say. I have observed as much," Cait said, enjoying the moment. Spending time with him there that afternoon was like a gift.

"Ye are a good woman Cait. It would be an honor if ye would accept my courtship."

"I-I…" She wanted to accept, to think he was sincere. Yet her mind and heart conflicted with one another, and she was left without words.

However, she wanted one moment for herself. A selfish interlude that would belong to her alone. On impulse, she slid closer, leaned forward, and kissed him. Stuart needed no further prodding. His muscular arms came around her, pulling her close as he deepened the kiss.

His lips traveled from her mouth down to her neck. Cait gasped when he kissed a trail to the top of her breasts, pushing them from below so that they were exposed.

She slid her hand under his tunic enjoying the feel of his warm skin. It was bold; but at the same time, she was possessed by a need she didn't understand. Cait tugged the fabric upward and Stuart removed it.

He remained still as she ran her fingers across the expanse of his bare chest and then down the center over a thin trail of hair.

Stuart was magnificent.

Once again, he took her mouth and guided Cait to her back and he lay beside her. As they continued to kiss, they became entangled. Her leg over his. His between hers. Their hands discovering all they could of each other.

Moments later, Cait's top was untied and her breasts free. Stuart covered them with kisses, sucking the tips into his mouth sending her to heights she never knew existed. She was aware there was more to come, and she craved it.

She gasped with delight when Stuart's hand slid under her skirts and up her leg. The calloused palm sending waves of sensations up her body and back down to between her legs. There it pooled into a delicious molten heat that needed sating.

"Oh," she whispered into his ear, nibbling at the lobe with quiet desperation. His soft moan telling her he enjoyed what she was doing. Emboldened, she licked down the side of his neck, loving the salty taste of his skin.

"Cait," he whispered, turning his head, and taking her mouth. When his tongue delved into her mouth, she loved the intrusion.

Her breath caught as he ran his fingers up her inner thigh. It was too much. She could faint from so many sensations at once. And yet, she urged him to take more.

AT FIRST, SHE wasn't sure what to think as Stuart slid his fingers between the folds of her sex. The touch jolted her and she tensed. When he repeated the movements, she was lost and gave into what would come next.

Every nerve in her body tingled with anticipation and she clung to him wanting to feel more, the need insatiable.

His harsh breaths combined with his touch was so unbearably wonderful that she cried out. Thankfully, his mouth covered hers in time to quiet the sound.

"Stuart," Cait gasped. "I cannot withstand more. I-I . . ."

It was as if she fell to pieces, broke apart into fragments of herself that would never return to their proper places.

In that moment, she was forever changed.

# CHAPTER ELEVEN

CAIT LEANED BACK against him as they rode to the keep. Every few minutes, he pressed a kiss to the top of her head.

"Will ye wait for me to come back for ye?" he asked for the third or fourth time. He purposely kept his mount to a slow pace, not wanting to stop being with her. "I leave in the morning."

She turned and looked up at him. "So soon?"

Just looking into her eyes made him want to change his plans and say to the devil with his quest for finding a place in the world. It was with her that he wished to be.

"I will not hold ye to anything because of what happened between us. We were not fully…intimate."

Once again, he kissed her, this time on her temple. "Aye not fully, but as much as I dare without yer brother killing me."

When she chuckled, it was light and airy.

"It is the first time I've heard ye laugh," he told her. "I want to spend a lifetime hearing that sound."

She tugged at the reins making the horse stop. "I would have never taken ye for someone so romantic." Her lips curved and there was warmth in her gaze when her eyes met his. "Everyone is urging me to go with ye and I will consider it while ye are gone. But once ye are settled, if I come to ye, it will be to accept the position of housekeeper."

He was silent, so she continued, "What happened between us this day, we must forget about it. Once I come to work for ye, I will need ye to allow me to do my duties and that is all."

"Ye will not work as a servant. I will speak to yer brother, and I will inform my family that ye are now to be considered part of the family."

By the rounding of her eyes, this was not what she expected. It was further confirmed when she slid from the horse and began pacing.

Stuart dismounted. "Cait?"

She held her hands up motioning him to keep his distance and then covered her mouth. "What are ye saying? Ye cannot say that. It is embarrassing. They will think I am yer lover."

At first, he wasn't sure what she meant, then it dawned. She thought he was to take her as mistress.

"I am an idiot." Stuart went to her and took her hands from her face. "I mean to marry ye, Cait."

The sharp pain at first didn't register. His shin burned from the swift kick. "Ouch."

"Ye cannot simply make an announcement like that. Be ye my superior or not." Cait blew out a breath. "Do not say things because ye feel the need to. I promise I will be fine."

Her stance straightened and chin lifted, she met his gaze with authority. "Stuart Ross, what do ye mean by all this?"

He'd never seen her so convicted in something. It was hard not to smile. This was exactly what he wanted. The quiet softness that hid an internal strength that would keep him in his place. Only a woman could be so multifaceted. Keeping a man guessing and discovering more of her with each passing day.

When he lowered to his knee, her eyes widened. Despite her demand, it was obvious she'd not expected this.

"Cait…" He suddenly realized he didn't know her surname. He would find out later. "Will ye do me the honor of becoming my wife?"

For a long moment, she stared at him. As the seconds passed, he began to second-guess himself. Had he done something wrong?

"Brown. My surname is Brown," she said, and then seeming to realize he remained on bended knee, she gasped. "Aye, Stuart Ross, I will marry ye."

He rose and wrapped her in his arms, turning in a circle as his heart beat so hard inside his chest, he thought it would burst through.

"I promise ye to do what I can to make ye happy—always." When she lowered her head and kissed him, all became right in his world.

THE REST OF the ride to the keep, they discussed what to do next. Stuart would first speak to Torac and then to his brothers. He asked Cait to wait for him in the kitchen and he would come fetch her. The announcement had to be made first to his family before any of the staff were told.

She nodded silently, seeming to take everything in.

"Here," he said placing his crest pin in her palm. "Keep it for me. To ensure ye know I mean every word."

He'd pinned it to his waist to be sure he had it when he left. But now it would serve a far better purpose. Ensuring Cait did not lose hope that he'd return as soon as he could for her.

"When will we marry?" she asked as the keep came into view.

"Upon my return."

Cait nodded and straightened, no longer leaning into him as they passed through the gates.

UPON DISMOUNTING AND helping her down, Stuart led his horse to the stables, sending the lads who came to help away. He needed the time to consider how best to approach Torac and explain to him that he'd proposed to Cait. The man was not one to be toyed with, of that Stuart was well aware. However, he was also a good warrior and valued member of the Ross guards.

Once he'd brushed his steed and filled its oat bucket, Stuart felt ready to speak to the warrior.

Torac was in the guard quarters sitting alone on a bench. It was as if the warrior was deep in thought but upon noticing Stuart's approach he stood.

Stuart motioned for him to sit and lowered to the bench next to him. It was best, in his opinion to speak about such things in a more relaxed manner.

"Ye seem deep in thought?" Stuart began. "Is there something amiss with the men?"

Torac shrugged. "There are always things amiss. But nothing that I cannot handle." The man slid him a look. "Is there something ye wish to speak about?"

"Aye, there is. I wish to inform ye that I have asked yer sister, to marry me."

Torac was silent, his gaze straight ahead. "I have only

known Cait a short while. She is sweet and susceptible. Do ye really mean to marry her?"

"I do," Stuart said. "I have grown to care for her and with my upcoming departure, I wanted to ensure she waited for me."

"I see." Torac let out a long breath. "I will not stand yer way. It is strange for me to take responsibility for a lass I barely know. However, I will demand that ye maintain boundaries until after the vows are spoken."

"I leave tomorrow…" Stuart began, but Torac interrupted.

"More the reason."

It took a moment for Stuart to reign in his temper and keep from snapping at the man, who seemed to insinuate that he'd take advantage of Cait just because he was leaving. Upon consideration, he could see how Torac was right in thinking it. In truth, he'd considered finding time alone with her that night. Not to make love, he would not take things so far, just to spend more time together.

"I give ye my word. I will respect yer wishes."

Torac stood and Stuart followed. When the man held out his hand, he took it, and they shook.

"Are ye sure there isn't anything I can help with?" Stuart asked.

Cait's brother looked past him toward the house. "All is well."

"I see," Stuart replied, not quite believing him. "Ye are a good warrior and have served my brother well."

Walking away, Stuart felt as if a weight was lifted from his shoulders. It seemed like everything was falling into its proper place now that he'd taken charge of his future.

Upon entering the house, he walked into the great room. Though not as full as usual, it was evident by the people mingling about that it would take most of the day for his brother to conclude his business after the midday meal.

Stuart walked past and down the corridor to find his mother, but she was not in the parlor, or in the upstairs sitting room.

"They are all in the dining room," a maid informed him.

"Good." He turned and headed to the dining room where he found they were all present: each of his brothers, their wives, and his mother. Before anyone could speak, he held up one finger. "Just a moment."

Stuart dashed from the dining room to the kitchen. Greer gave him a confused look. "Yer mother is waiting for ye in the dining room."

"Aye, I saw her," he replied.

Other than Greer and two other women who were placing items on trays, no one else was about. He peered into the small alcove where the servants took their meals. It was empty.

"Where is Cait?" he asked looking to Greer.

"Went to fetch water," Greer replied motioning to the door that led to the courtyard. "Goodness Mister Stuart, what is all the fuss about?"

He blew out a breath. "No matter what Cait says. From now on, do not ask her to do anything. Am I clear?"

Greer's face lit up. "Very much so."

"What does that mean?" As he walked out, he heard one of the maids ask.

Cait walked back from the well with two buckets, one in each hand. Her expression was serene until she spotted him.

An adorable blush brightened her cheeks. "I will take these to the kitchen and then we can…"

She stopped midsentence when he grabbed the pails and practically ran to the house. "What are ye doing?" she asked hurrying to catch up.

Water sloshed over the sides of the buckets when he placed them none-so-gently on the floor just inside the kitchen.

Then he took Cait's arm. "My family is in the dining room. We are to announce our betrothal."

"Oh, no." Cait pulled her arm from his grasp and covered her cheeks with both hands. "I cannot possibly face them. I am too nervous." She smoothed her hair and apron, then hastily took it off and hung it on a peg.

Stuart let out a breath. "I leave in the morning. It must be today." Once again, he took her arm and tugged her forward.

Upon reentering the dining room, everyone looked at him.

"Cait and I have an announcement," Stuart said. Smiling he looked to his right only to find that Cait was not beside him. He looked to the left and she was not there either.

"She's behind ye," his mother explained.

Taking a step to the side, he wrapped his arm around her waist and pulled Cait to stand beside him. "I asked Cait to marry me and she has agreed."

His mother and the other women's faces lit up and they jumped to their feet coming forward to hug him and then Cait, who remained halfway hidden behind him once again.

When his brothers approached, he moved away from her hoping the women would not let her escape.

"Congratulations, I wish ye the best," Darach said hugging him. Similar sentiments were repeated by Ewan, Duncan, and

Caelan.

"Ye may change yer mind in a moment," Gideon said cryptically before hugging him.

"This is wonderful news," his mother exclaimed, pulling Cait alongside. "Ye must join us for the meal." Her eyes twinkled when meeting his. "When do ye plan to marry? Tonight?"

Stuart had to laugh. His poor mother had become accustomed to impromptu, unplanned weddings. "Not until I return. There is plenty of time to plan a proper wedding."

His heart warmed when Cait's face brightened. "Nothing too elaborate."

"Oh dear," his mother's face registered alarm. "Where are my manners. We have a guest. Lila Maclean arrived just a few moments ago."

It was as if everything in the room moved slower. Every set of eyes in the room went from him to the woman who sat at the table.

In truth, Stuart had never seen someone so striking. With midnight black hair, olive skin, and bright grey eyes, she was an exotic beauty.

The woman's gaze moved from him to study Cait. Lila's gaze swept over Cait from head to toe and back again, then settled on him.

"Lila, this is my son, Stuart. The only one ye had yet to meet," his mother said.

Stuart nodded at the woman, feeling a bit disconcerted by the expectation on everyone's faces. Yes, he realized she had come to get to know him. Despite finding the woman exquisite, she did not appeal to him the way Cait did.

"Seems an opportune time for a betrothal," she said in a husky voice. There was disbelief in her gaze and something akin to disappointment. "I wish ye...both the best." She finally dragged her gaze from his and looked to Cait. It was obvious she found Cait's apparel lacking.

Stuart pulled a chair back and guided Cait to sit. She'd been stunned silent, but he was proud that she kept her gaze forward, not glancing away when Lila looked at her.

"Tell us Stuart, what are yer plans upon arriving on yer lands?" his mother asked a question they all knew the reply to. He understood it was for both Cait and Lila's benefit.

"Once we arrive, the first priority will be to ensure the house will provide refuge from the weather. It is imperative we can remain warm once winter sets. The fields will be cleared, but planting cannot take place until spring." Stuart continued to tell them the larger plans of building pens and corrals for the livestock, hiring helpers, and finally building a rapport with the villagers.

Everyone listened politely, every so often asking about something. He noted that Lila had lost all interest in anything he said and kept sliding looks to Cait.

# CHAPTER TWELVE

IT WAS THE most mortifying and awkward meal of her entire life. Cait could not figure out where to look, opting to keep her attention on Lady Mariel, who did her best to make her feel part of the conversation.

Stuart became preoccupied with discussing the logistics of his upcoming travel and though she didn't begrudge him his enthusiasm, it meant she was left to partake of the women's discussion. Thankfully, after a moment they turned their attention to Lila Maclean and asked about her home, family, and travel from the Isle of Skye.

The woman was breathtakingly beautiful. Her face was perfection with long dark lashes surrounding smoky grey eyes. And the darkest hair Cait had ever seen. Her clothing was impeccable; the emerald green color bringing out the depth of her olive skin.

There was a coolness in her eyes when looking at her. Every time Lila glanced in Cait's direction, she felt insignificant. How could Stuart choose her over a woman who was obviously more suited for him?

"What are yer plans while here?" Beatrice asked, obviously uninformed of the reason for Lila's travel.

The women went quiet, everyone's gazes went from Lila, to her, to Stuart. For an awkward moment, Cait considered stating that Lila was there to become betrothed to Stuart.

"I am here to learn the intricacies of maintaining ledgers," Lila said and then added. "Who is to take me on, I am not sure about." Her husky laugh lightened the mood.

Isobel was quick to reassure the woman. "Caelan and I will tutor ye and ye will be prepared to take on yer family's ledgers in no time at all."

"I appreciate yer kindness. I know my brother sprung this on yer husband quickly. I was actually quite surprised when the reply came agreeing that I come."

Lila and Isobel continued talking about household accounts. Taking advantage of the distraction, Lady Mariel leaned into Cait's ear. "Once we get ye established in yer own bedchamber, we will see about better clothing and whatever else ye will need."

Cait could not stop the heat that traveled from her chest to her face. Unlike someone like Lila, she would have to be provided for by Stuart's family. Everything from dresses to shoes because she could scarcely afford more than a hand-me-down chemise.

"Perhaps I should remain in the cottage with my mother and brother for now," Cait said not wishing for Lila to witness Stuart's family having to expend the energy to ensure she could properly represent them.

"Come," Lady Mariel took her hand.

Stuart turned to them and his mother gave him a quick smile. "We have to attend to something. She will be all yers in a moment."

They walked out and Lady Mariel ushered Cait through the great hall, up the stairs, and into the sitting room.

"I imagine ye feel a bit out of sorts with everything," Lady Mariel stated, looking to the door as a maid entered.

"Can I get something for ye Lady Mariel?" the young girl asked, her gaze sliding to Cait for a scant second. It was long enough for Cait to notice her curiosity and possibly fodder for gossip.

Lady Mariel motioned to the girl. "Please fetch some warm cider."

The maid hurried away, and Lady Mariel returned her attention to Cait. "Ye will grow used to it. Understand that there must be a time of adjustment. When ye accepted Stuart's proposal, ye had to have known."

"In truth. I barely thought of anything. Ye think it is a mistake." Cait didn't form it as a question, but more as a statement. It was obvious Lady Mariel herself was accessing how best to handle the current situation.

"Stuart is smitten with ye and I wish for my sons to be happy and their choice in who they marry is theirs alone."

The reply did not make Cait feel better. She wished to disappear, return to her cottage and start the day over. This time, she'd say no to Stuart.

"I will inform him that I will not marry him," Cait said standing. "I simply cannot embarrass yer family like this." Her heart broke in that moment. Tears stung her eyes.

She loved Stuart. She hadn't realized it until this moment. She truly did love him. When he'd asked her to marry him, it had been the singular happiest moment of her life. And now not only would she hurt him, but she and her family would be forced to leave.

Lady Mariel glared at her. "Ye must not love my son."

"I do," Cait replied emphatically. "I love him."

"Then why do ye give up so easily? My son deserves a woman who will fight for him and not allow scorn from a simple maid to put her off."

Properly chastised, Cait lowered back to sit. "Ye are right." Closing her eyes, Cait inhaled deeply once and then again. With each breath, she sat up taller until her back was ramrod straight. When she opened her eyes, she met Lady Mariel's gaze directly.

"I will make Stuart proud every day, and once we marry, I will do my best to be a good wife and partner."

Lady Mariel's lips curved. "That is what I hoped to hear." She looked to the door just as the maid returned holding a tray with two cups.

The maid placed the tray on a side table.

Cait met the maid's gaze. "Not there, put it here on this one." She motioned to another table that was between her and Lady Mariel.

The maid was astonished at Cait's firm tone and looked to Lady Mariel, who remained silent. Once the young woman moved the tray, the girl looked to Cait. "Is there anything else ye require…?"

"Miss Cait," Lady Mariel said. "No, thank ye."

"Let us find something more appropriate for ye to wear. There are clothes here that Ella left behind. Ye are a bit shorter, but about the same size as my daughter. Once that is done, ye must spend some time with Stuart. Find out if there is anything he wishes ye to acquire while he is gone. I will see to things such as learning to manage household accounts," she paused before looking to Cait innocently. "Perhaps ye can learn alongside Lila."

Despite the situation, they both chuckled.

They finished the cider and went to Ella's bedchamber. After a few moments, several skirts, blouses, vests, and other clothes were in a neat pile on the bed for Cait. Cora was summoned and she helped Cait change and brush her hair up into a simple bun.

"This is most exciting," Cora said. "I will definitely go with ye to yer new home once it is time. I am so very happy for ye."

They hugged and Cait wiped a tear from her cheek. "Ye are a true friend, Cora. Thank ye. I am excited that ye will come with me."

She'd changed into a dark brown skirt, pale tan blouse, and flowered vest. On her feet, Cait wore simple brown boots. When she peered into the looking glass, her breath caught at the woman who looked back at her.

"It is me?" Cait asked looking to Cora. "I look so different."

"Like a proper lady," Cora replied. "Now, ye must seek out Mister Stuart. He must be anxious to spend time with ye."

Her stomach in knots, Cait descended the stairs and went in search of Stuart. When she walked into the parlor, she found him standing at the large windows with his brother, Caelan, looking out to the sea.

Unsure if she should interrupt, Cait almost turned around. Then remembering Lady Mariel's words, she cleared her throat instead.

Both men turned, their gazes approving as they took her in. "If I may interrupt for a bit," she said.

Caelan motioned to Stuart. "He is all yers." The man gave her a warm smile and walked out.

"Ye look very pretty," Stuart said closing the distance between them and kissing her soundly. "I am not sure I can leave ye behind."

"I can go with ye…"

"No, I will not have ye working there. Besides, ye told me yer mother needs ye here."

Cait hated that they'd be apart so soon after becoming betrothed. "Very well. I will support ye from here and do what I can to help." Cait laid her head on his chest, the feel of him so comforting, she wanted to cry at the thought he'd be gone the next day.

"I will miss ye," she admitted. "It is much too soon for ye to leave. We have only just begun to truly get to know one another."

"I agree," he said holding her close. "However, if I put it off one day, then it will turn into another and another. It is best that I proceed as planned. Besides, it is not so far that I cannot come and visit every fortnight or so."

Her heart lightened. "I'd not thought about that."

"Be sure to go to the seamstress to get clothes made. Once the house is habitable, ye will have to come prepared with all the necessary items for it. Ye should begin acquiring items such as…" He stopped and frowned down at her. "Whatever it is that is needed for a house."

Cait laughed. "I will ask yer mother for help."

"Good."

"There is something else," Stuart said, placing his curled forefinger under her chin and lifting it. "I am as surprised by Lila Maclean's appearance as ye are. Do not fret over it. I am sure Caelan, and Isobel will keep her busy. If anything, I expect that she will stay at Caelan's house and not here."

"I can tell she was disappointed that ye were not available for courtship," Cait said. "Stuart, if ye have any doubts after seeing her, I would not blame ye…"

"Not one single doubt."

His mouth covered hers and she clung to him in a desperate attempt to not only prolong the kiss, but to memorize every second. The hardness of his body. His scent. How his kisses tasted. The low rumble that rose from his chest as he deepened the kiss. And the way his strong hands roamed over her back.

The wonder of discovery between them promised so much more and Cait wished the moment to never end. Parting her lips, she accepted the intrusion of his tongue past them. She suckled on it timidly at first and then with greed. His hands moved from her sides to cup her breasts, his thumbs circling the sensitive tips.

"Oh, Stuart," Cait gasped out the words.

"Mmmm," he replied trailing his lips from hers down the side of her neck. "I desire ye so very much."

He lifted his head and peered down at her. "Why did I agree to wait to marry?" His crooked smile melted her heart.

Before Cait could form a reply, once again his mouth took hers.

"Ye must promise to come for me," Cait said stopping the kiss. "Promise."

Stuart studied her face, his brows drawn together. "Why do ye ask? I have asked ye to marry me. I pledge my love to ye, of course I will return."

Swallowing past the lump that formed, Cait looked away to

the view outside. The waves crashed against the shore in a reassuring pattern that promised another would come soon.

"I cannot yet believe this all to be true," Cait admitted. "It is like a dream that ye would want someone like me for a wife."

Stuart took her shoulders. "Cait, it is only the circumstance of our birth that makes us different. It could have been the opposite. Would ye have considered me less than ye?"

"I do not know. I cannot answer that question," she answered honestly. "However, when I look into yer eyes, I do see that ye care."

"Look at me," Stuart commanded. When she did, he locked gazes with her. "I give ye my word to return and marry ye."

Cait released a long breath and as a tear trickled down her cheek. "I wish ye did not have to leave. At the same time, I look forward to starting a new life with ye away from here. It will be easier not to have to be over the servants who I worked alongside with."

"I agree," Stuart said. "Now let us see about my packing. Will ye help me?"

They entered his bedchamber where Anton and another servant were packing. Stuart pointed to some things and then instructed that many be left behind.

"I will take the rest of my things when I return."

Cait walked through the room and lowered to a chair where she watched the proceedings. Instinctively, she knew they'd spend every minute together until bedtime.

Once the trunks were packed and carried downstairs, Cora entered with a tray. "Some honeyed mead and toasted bread," she announced placing the tray on a small table.

Stuart lowered to the chair opposite Cait. "Tell me, what do ye think yer mother's reaction will be?"

"I'd not thought about it. She will be very happy for us."

"Ensure she and yer brother come to live here at the keep. I will not rest if I think of ye traipsing through the forest alone." He gave her a stern look and then his expression softened. "Please."

"I will ensure it as soon as possible. My brother is interested in working with horses…"

"He can apprentice at our new home. For now, he can work here. I will ensure to speak to the stable master in the morning." He drank the mead and bit the toast.

Cait watched him for a long moment. It was incredible to her to sit across from the laird's brother, who was now her betrothed. At the same time it felt relaxed and comfortable to sit and share toast. "What do ye think yer family thinks of our betrothal?"

For a moment he considered her question, the entire time his gaze on her. "My brothers are not surprised. I do not believe mother to be either. Darach was the first one to ask what my intentions were."

Cait was surprised and even more at his next statement.

"I spoke to Torac and informed him of our betrothal."

"Ye are thorough." Cait couldn't help but chuckle.

Stuart stood and took her hands pulling her to stand. They walked to the window and he wrapped his arms around her. After pressing a kiss to her lips, he turned her to look out and pointed.

"I will be in that direction, beyond the trees."

For a long time, they stood with his arms around her. Cait closed her eyes praying the closeness they felt in that moment would remain when separate from each other.

THE NEXT MORNING, Cait stood beside Lady Mariel and Lady Isobel as they wished the caravan of travelers farewell.

Leading the group was Stuart, accompanied by Ewan, who'd agreed to go for a short while and help get things set up.

Cait waved enthusiastically and wore a bright smile when Stuart turned to her. They'd stayed up until quite late talking and making plans for a future together, and she hoped he wasn't too tired for the trip.

As they rode away, she did her best to push away any worries. Stuart had reassured her he'd return as often as possible. Upon waking her first thought was that Stuart Ross was her betrothed. It was still so very hard to believe.

"Let us go inside and do something to keep yer mind away from sadness," Lady Mariel said. "I do believe there are many tasks that require our attention."

By the end of the first day, Cait collapsed into her bed exhausted from keeping up with Lady Mariel and spending time with Greer going over the menu for the week. She'd asked Lady Mariel for kitchen duties as it was where she felt most comfortable.

She'd been installed in Ella's old bedchamber, which felt both intrusive and reassuring that she was now considered part of the family. When she'd spoken to Lady Mariel about her family. It was decided that her mother was to be moved to a bedchamber near the servant's quarters and Brice would be housed in the guard's quarters with Torac.

Looking up at the ceiling, Cait considered how different her life had become and how many more changes were on the way. Her eyes became heavy, but before she could let herself sleep, she slid from the bed and kneeled next to it to pray for Stuart's safety.

# CHAPTER THIRTEEN

IT WAS LATE in the day when they arrived at Stuart's lands. The sun was low in the horizon causing the trees to cast long shadows across the field that surrounded a house that had barely survived the passage of time.

"I am not sure it is habitable," Ewan said looking to Stuart. "I think we should set up camp and get settled. We can take our time exploring the structure once the sun rises." Ewan would remain for a few weeks but planned to leave before the winter settled in. Artair would come and replace him then.

Stuart agreed and scanned the area for a place that would be suitable. What had once been fields were now overgrown, young trees and bushes covering the ground. There were a few places that were passable for camping, but it would take them until nightfall to clear any space.

"This will take a while," Stuart said turning his horse around so he could address the small group.

Stuart looked to the men, who also scanned the area. Some wary, others with interest.

"We will choose somewhere not too far from the house to clear and set up camp. First, we need to make proper shelters, so we don't have to worry about the elements as we work to restore the house."

Ewan added, "There are plenty of young trees we can use

to make sturdy shelters. It should not take overly long to cut them down." He gave his brother a challenging look. "Two each?"

He and Ewan often competed at everything. Most times, neither won because they were so close in size and stature.

"Very well," Ewan said pointing to a narrow path. "Let's try this way. Hopefully, the carts will fit through."

It took several hours to get to the spot they'd chosen. Ewan got what he wished for because they had to chop down more than two young trees each, to get the wagons through.

By the time they were able to clear not only the path, but an area for the shelters, it was dark. They worked by torchlight to erect two tents made from linen that had been covered in fat before allowing to dry. The fabric was tough and would provide shelter from the wind and light rain.

While the men worked, Dougal set up a separate shelter for himself and his wife. He made a sturdy structure from the fallen trees adding a leather roof.

Everyone was exhausted as they quickly ate pottage and drank ale, anxious to sleep.

Stuart lifted the flap of the tent and searched for a space to lie down. He, his brother, and Anton would share this one, while the rest of the men were in the other.

Once he settled on the pallet of blankets, he promptly fell asleep.

A loud conversation startled Stuart awake the next morning. Thankfully, it looked to be a sunny day. Unfortunately, the bright light coming through the tent meant he'd overslept.

He made quick work of pulling on his boots and walked out to find that a group of men had arrived and were arguing with Ewan who looked half asleep and fully annoyed.

When his brother turned to him, he motioned for Stuart to hurry closer.

“These men came to challenge our being here. They say this land belongs to the village constable,” Ewan informed him in a bored tone. “I suppose we must go and meet this man.”

“No need,” a burly man holding a wooden club said. “Here ’e comes now.”

A man rode toward them atop a black horse. By the way he sat in the saddle, he considered himself to be quite important. Stuart glanced over his shoulder at his own warhorse, which would dwarf the man’s.

“Why are ye on my land?” the man called out. “Leave at once or I will set my men upon ye.”

Stuart looked to his own men who approached.

“Mount and bring our steeds,” he ordered in a low tone. It was but a short moment later that the men returned and brought their horses. Both Ewan and Stuart mounted at once.

At seeing the horses and Stuart’s guards on mounts, the burly villager and his companions exchanged concerned looks, especially when the guards drew their swords.

Stuart pulled out his tartan that hung from a sack on his saddle and threw it over one shoulder. “Who are ye?” he said meeting the man’s gaze.

At seeing the tartan, the man became less assured. “I am Torridon St. Claire, the constable of the nearby village.”

Stuart knew the man made up the surname. He was most probably a Smith, but he let it pass. “I am Stuart Ross, this is my brother Ewan Ross, my cousin Dougal Ross,” he motioned to each man as he spoke. “This land, as well as the village ye all live in, belong to Clan Ross."

The constable's eyes narrowed. "Why should we believe ye or that ye care about our village. Laird Ross has not stepped foot near here in years. We have had to fend fer ourselves and do not require ye or any of yer family to come now and take what has become ours."

Obviously, the man and villagers were not aware of his father's death. Stuart considered that perhaps now was not the best time to inform them of the fact.

He looked from the self-appointed leader to the men that had arrived on foot. "I do not come to take anything from ye. I come to settle on my land where I will farm and raise livestock. There will be work for those needing it."

At his words, the men's expressions became eager, and they showed great interest.

"We do need work," one said.

"Will ye pay?" another asked.

"Yer father made us work without recompense. I do not trust ye," another added.

There were murmurs of agreement. Ewan gave Stuart an urging look.

"My father, Laird Ross, is dead. My brother, Darach Ross, is now laird of Clan Ross. Ye will find him to be a good and fair leader."

Two younger men turned and raced away, no doubt wishing to be the first to take the news to the village. They would have plenty to share, Stuart mused.

There was a strange interchange between the constable and the gathered men. It was as if they were fearful.

"Return to the village, I will deal with this," Torridon ordered, his voice held a menacing tone. "Do not trust anything ye heard."

Ewan along with two guardsmen guided their horses around the group, blocking them from leaving. Once again, the men looked to the constable for guidance.

"Ye are no one to give orders," Stuart said. "I am of a mind to imprison ye for yer insolence."

"Ye have no such authority." The constable glared at him. "We are our own people now."

It was a turn of events Stuart had not expected. Guiding his horse closer to the constable, he lowered his voice and met the man's gaze. "What do ye hope to achieve by goading me? I can have an army triple the size of the village here in two days. Do not try me on this."

The constable's gaze slipped away first, his brows lowering. "I only state the truth. Ye can try to do what ye wish, but soon ye will discover that the people here do not trust ye and will never respect ye."

The man turned his horse around, effectively ending the conversation. "Come," he called out to the men, who hurried past Ewan and the guards to walk back to the village.

"Should we stop them?" Dougal asked coming alongside Stuart. "That is going to be a problem."

"Aye," Stuart replied. "I will need able men to help clear the land and to work on the house. My brother will be sending the animals in a fortnight and we'll need help with them as well."

Ewan motioned to the house. "First priority is fortifying the house. Worry about the village once the work here is completed. Meanwhile, we can send a message back to Darach to send more men to help clear the land."

THE OUTER STRUCTURE of the house was in good shape. A few windows had to be replaced and mortar added to some bricks to ensure it was weatherproofed, but it would not be a lot of work.

The interior was another story completely. Only a couple of the walls and hearths were usable. They would have to rebuild walls, stairs, doors, and furniture. The front entrance was flanked by two large windows, quite rare for homes of the time. There was a large main room that led to a second room of about the same size. There was an archway that led to a kitchen and a second corridor where three smaller rooms were. Stuart guessed they'd been used for servant sleeping quarters. Off the kitchen was a back exit to what he assumed used to be a garden.

To the right of the main room was a corridor that led to three bedchambers.

He turned to Ewan. "Who lived here?"

His brother shrugged. "After our grandfather died, I do not think anyone has for at least twenty years."

He believed it from the looks of it. Rats scurried from the hearth when they entered what looked to be a good-sized kitchen. Of all the rooms, this one would have to be dealt with first.

Pushing on the thick support wooden posts, he was glad to note they remained strong.

"There is much to do," a feminine voice said, and they

turned to see that a pair of women accompanied Dougal's wife, Bree.

One of the women straightened her cap and gave Stuart a straight look. "I am Maisie, this is my sister, Grace. We will have this kitchen set up in no time at all."

Grace's face brightened with a smile that showcased missing teeth. "We worked for yer grandfather, bless his soul."

Not about to stand between three women and whatever they had planned, Stuart and Ewan motioned to the kitchen. "See about whatever is needed."

The women bustled past them.

"Strange," Stuart said when they'd returned to the largest room at the front of the house. "The women do not seem affected by the constable."

"It could be they do not live in the village or have no reason to fear him."

"The men did seem to fear him," Stuart said.

His brother nodded.

They went outside to find men clearing brush from around the house, and one sat on a fallen tree forming makeshift brooms.

Ewan looked around and smiled. "I do believe ye will have a good place to live. I almost envy ye."

Two men came through the trees with buckets of water and headed into the house. Ewan went to a wagon and returned with hammers. He motioned to the man making brooms. "See about cleaning out the hearths."

Stuart decided his first task would be to build a ladder so he could make repairs to the roof.

And so, the work that would take them many weeks to

complete had begun.

ONE MORNING STUART woke ready to face the long list of tasks to be completed that day and realized with so many things requiring his attention every day he'd lost track of exactly what day it was.

Walking out of the bedchamber—he'd only moved into the day before—he went to the kitchen. There he found the sisters, Maisie and Grace, busily cooking a simple fare of eggs and porridge.

"The hens laid plenty of eggs," Maisie said with excitement. "They have finally settled. We only took half of the eggs and put the others in a separate pen. Soon we'll have plenty of chickens."

Stuart settled into a small table that had been set up just outside the kitchen. The clearing of land to build corrals for the livestock had taken priority over the building of furniture, so the house still remained mostly bare.

First and last meal were the only time he sat and rested, the remainder of the time he had too many tasks to take breaks. This day however, he didn't feel a need to hurry.

"Why are ye not scared of the constable? Some of the villagers seem to fear him?" Stuart asked the women.

The women exchanged looks, seeming to gauge what to say. Finally, Grace met his gaze as she slid him a bowl of porridge with a fried egg on top. "Torridon is a cruel sort, who takes glee in making people's lives miserable. Since we've always lived away from the village, he hasn't bothered us much."

"Why do the people obey his every command then?" Stuart said taking a spoonful of food, blowing on it, and then eating it. It was quite delicious.

Maisie was first to reply. "Because the man has been smart about how he controls everyone. If he can't get them through loans that require higher payments in return, he gets information about 'em they don't want gettin' out. And he also has himself a group of evil doers that follow his orders and threaten people who don't obey him."

"Those were the ones who came here the first day ye arrived," Grace added.

Stuart nodded. "Aye, they seemed to obey his every command."

It would be easy enough to rectify the situation. He had to get rid of the constable. Since Ewan was to depart the next day, he'd ask his brother to ride with him into the village to get a better idea of what the situation was.

THE SEASIDE VILLAGE consisted of a scattering of cottages on hilly land. Most of the thatched roof homes faced the sea, a true testament to the people's regard for where their livelihood came from. There were a few shops that had been lined up on a road that curved around an inlet. The rest were small homes. Several people milled about, some on foot, others urging slow mules to pull their wagons. In the water was a smattering of boats from which Stuart guessed men fished.

Altogether, he had to admit, it was a beautiful place. The

salty air reminded him of home, and he wondered if he should have moved into the house closer to the village. Perhaps he would in the future. For now, he would have to ride the hour or so it took to see about the villagers.

When he rode past a small home, two barefoot children ran out and stared at him. Lifting tiny hands to block the sun from their eyes, their rounded eyes took in his horse.

"Are ye a warrior?" the lad asked his eyes moving from his face to the horse.

"I am Stuart Ross, I live near here," he replied and smiled down at the child.

"I think ye is a warrior," a young girl standing next to the boy insisted.

Stuart reached into his purse and pulled out a pair of coins tossing them to the delighted children, who picked them up and raced into the house.

He continued until reaching the main road and dismounted. In truth, his horse was quite large and intimidating. The animal was at home on the battlefield, fearless and trained to trample the enemy. Not exactly the type of horse to make people feel at ease.

Ewan met his gaze. "I like the place. I think it suits ye."

Turning to the horse, he patted the animal's head twice. It was a command to keep its head bent and give an illusion of meekness. The horse snorted to communicate its annoyance but did as commanded.

Pulling the horse behind, Stuart walked to the first shop. It was a bakery. The man behind the counter started at seeing him and rushed to the door. "Mister Stuart. I wondered how long it would be before ye came to the village." The man gave a slight bow. "I am Albert Smith."

Stuart took advantage of the fact that the man seemed pleased to see him. "How are things here at the moment? I heard there was a problem with yer livestock."

"Aye, it was quite horrible. We lost almost all the cows, except for the few that belong to the constable. Managed to save most of the sheep, which is good."

"Do the sheep belong to the constable as well?" Stuart eyed the man, noticing he'd become nervous.

"I am not sure." The baker seemed to realize he should probably not be having this conversation. "Can I gift ye some bread?"

Stuart accepted several loaves but insisted on paying. The baker was a likable man and Stuart informed him that there was work available if he knew of men needing it.

Continuing, the next shop he stopped at was a cobbler. The man sat outside his shop, leather atop a form as he worked without looking up. Despite the man pretending not to notice him, Stuart had seen him looking over when he'd been speaking to the baker.

This man was slight, with thinning hair and he moved quickly giving the impression of someone who was always nervous.

"I am Stuart Ross…"

"I am well aware Mister Stuart," the man interrupted. "Welcome." Still, he did not look up, his hands smoothing down the leather.

"Why are the villagers so scared of the constable?" Stuart asked knowing it would startle the man.

His question had the desired effect. The man's eyes rounded, and he looked in the direction of a large house in the distance. "We are not scared of him."

"That is not the impression I get. Tell me. What do ye think of him?"

This time the man's hands dropped down to the tabletop. "He is a strong man, who ensures the village has order."

"Order," Stuart said then looked to the house. He remembered it. When he was a child, he'd visited his great uncle and great aunt, who'd lived there. The house belonged to his family. Had his father gifted it to the constable? Somehow, he doubted it.

Then again if it was empty, it was better to put it to use.

Stuart considered that it could possibly be a better location for him and Cait. He'd have to ask her where she preferred to live.

"Order should be maintained by a constable. However, it is not his position to take from those he is sworn to protect." Stuart met the man's gaze. "A good and fair man does not rule by fear."

The cobbler nodded. "I am Roger McTernan," the man said standing and giving a slight bow. "Welcome, Laird."

*Laird.* The word hung in the air. Stuart nodded in return and continued on.

# CHAPTER FOURTEEN

CAIT LOOKED UP from her embroidery when her mother walked into the parlor. Each time she saw her mother, Clara, now, she was struck at the difference. Not only had her health improved dramatically, but in clothes of better quality, she looked every bit a lady.

"I was searching for ye," her mother said settling into a chair, her face automatically looking out to the view. "Ye have kept to yerself for a few days now. Lady Mariel is worried."

For a moment, she considered her words. "I do not belong here, Mother. Stuart is not going to return. What will happen to us then?"

"Ye worry overmuch," her mother protested. "In the last message, Stuart informed ye of how much there was still to do. It is obvious he has been delayed."

Cait shook her head. "Already the entire season has passed. Winter has set in and with it comes the rainy season making travel difficult."

To ignore the silence, she began embroidering again. It was a simple design that Lady Mariel had taught her. Dainty flowers and leaves, in a chain pattern. As well as embroidery, a tutor had been hired to teach her to read and write. She'd taken to both quickly, soaking in as much as she could on the chance she'd be forced to leave and start anew.

Knowing how to read and write would make it possible for her to hire on as a governess or assist in running a household. She'd shadowed both Lady Mariel and Lady Isobel, watching and learning every single aspect of running a keep. Although she wasn't sure how large the home Stuart owned was, she would be prepared to ensure everything would be taken care of.

Already weeks had passed since the last time a missive had come from him. His brothers, Duncan and Gideon, had both visited and returned with news of the progress being made on the lands and home.

Each time they'd brought a letter for her. In each letter, Stuart wrote of what he did, promised to return soon so they could marry, and then explained all the work yet to be done.

"If the house is ready, there is only one reason for him not to return for me Mother." Cait finally put into words the fear that had filled her in the last days. "He's changed his mind and hopes I realize it and grant him his freedom."

"Nonsense," her mother said. "He was visibly smitten with ye."

"He has been gone longer than the time we've spent together. I sincerely doubt he misses me. How can he?"

Her mother took her in. "Is it ye that has had a change of heart?"

Cait met her mother's eyes. "Honestly? Yes. I am beginning to question my feelings. I have not seen him, have only had letters…" Her breath caught, a dark sensation gripped her chest. "Father promised to return. He lied to us. Never returned." She had to take a deep breath and wiped an errant tear. "Do you not see Mother?"

"Ye have his family's support. He proposed to ye and announced it to the entire family including his brother, the laird." Her mother's eyes shined with unshed tears. "He is not yer father. Stuart Ross will not step back from his responsibility to ye."

"And yet he has Mother. He can take years and not return for me. No one can chastise him for it, as the only duty he has is to provide for me and that he has done."

Her mother balked, "Then ye should take matters in hand and travel to see him. Clear things up in yer mind. Sitting here worrying will only make ye more and more bitter."

"I am not bitter," Cait argued.

"Ye certainly are not sweet," her mother replied with a soft smile.

Just then Cora walked in. "The midday meal is ready."

WALKING INTO THE dining room with her mother made Cait think back to when she and Stuart had entered to announce their engagement and how awkward it had been.

Now it was an everyday occurrence. The simple midday meal of cheese, bread, and fruit was often a time when they would talk of plans for the following day.

Most times, the men did not attend and instead ate in the great hall while listening to clan grievances.

This time, however, Gideon and Caelan were there.

"Since Ewan has returned and is here to sit with Darach, I have excused myself to enjoy time with ye," Caelan told Lady Mariel.

Despite the fact his own mother lived not too far away, Caelan and Lady Mariel had a close relationship and he carved out time to spend with her.

"How are ye feeling?" Lady Mariel asked him, touching his cheek. "Ye are cool to the touch."

Caelan had recently been abed for over a week. The healer was not sure what illness it was, but he'd been feverish and without appetite. The handsome man looked well recovered now.

"Would ye like to go visit Beatrice with me tomorrow?" Isobel asked Cait. "We can stop at the village on the way there."

"Aye, I would enjoy it. Thank ye."

"Ye have to stop thanking me for everything," Isobel said with a light chuckle.

Cait let out a breath. It was time she told them her thoughts. "Ye are all so kind to me, and I will be forever grateful. I must admit to feeling as if I may never truly come to be a member of the family."

"I agree, my son has been gone overlong. But I know Stuart and he will do as he promised," Lady Mariel said and then looked to Caelan. "Do ye not agree that yer brother will return soon?"

"Knowing Stuart, he wants everything to be perfect before ye arrive to live there. If someone does not go and fetch him with a warning ye are changing yer mind, he will continue doing this and that, never fully satisfied."

"Cait is not changing her mind. She is worried however that he may have," her mother interjected in a soft voice.

"He has not," Lady Mariel assured them.

"Someone needs to go fetch him," Gideon said lowering his cup. "I can go."

"I will go," Caelan said. "Ye just returned from yer last trip."

Lady Mariel placed both hands on the table and looked to everyone there. "I do not care who goes, but someone must go and fetch Stuart. He has been gone too long."

Cait's eyes widened at the stir she'd caused. "I do not mean to cause discord."

"Ye are not," Isobel said patting her hand. "Despite their sense of honor and such, Ross men seem inclined to make ridiculous mistakes."

"Let us go speak to Darach, he will have to say who goes," Caelan said standing. Then as the brothers walked out, Gideon winked at her.

"When it's his turn, he may not be so jovial about it," Lady Mariel murmured shaking her head as she followed her youngest's progress.

"Now," Isobel said. "We should prepare for a wedding."

"Visit yer sister as planned. The day after tomorrow, we will go to the village and procure whatever is needed to decorate." Lady Mariel gave Cait an accessing look. "We may have to summon the seamstress. Ye have lost weight since yer wedding dress was made."

Annis, Isobel's companion, and Cora entered and joined in the conversation, along with Cait's mother. Everything that would be required for the wedding festivities was discussed, from food and drink to décor. It seemed with the two recent weddings, the women of Keep Ross had matters well in hand.

As the conversations whirled around Cait, she did her best to grasp the reality of the situation. Was she willing to marry a man who had to be fetched?

She held up a hand and everyone stopped speaking to look at her.

"If Stuart shows any inkling that he does not wish to be married, I will not force him into it. Perhaps we should wait until his arrival to make any preparations. I do not wish for ye to go to any more trouble for a wedding that may not take place."

"A RIDER CAME and Darach says he has a message for ye," Cora said entering Cait's bedchamber.

Despite Stuart's last written missive claiming his assurance of wishing to marry her, Cait could not help the sense of dread. Why had Darach not sent the letter with Cora?

"What do ye suppose it is? Usually, it is a written missive that he could have asked ye to give me."

Cora shrugged. "It is strange."

Taking her friend's hand, Cait made her way down the corridor and down the stairs to find the laird. He was in the great room, along with Caelan and Ewan, who didn't pay her much mind as she neared.

"Ah, there ye are," Darach said motioning for her to come closer. "The guard has a message for ye and Mother."

The sense of dread grew stronger. All Cait could think about was her mother and brother and what would happen if she had to leave.

A gruff guard stood with Lady Mariel next to the high board and Cait walked to them, still grasping Cora's hand. Neither the guard nor Lady Mariel seemed discomfited by

Cora's presence.

"Mister Stuart requests that ye come to visit his home and perhaps remain for winter season."

Lady Mariel frowned. "They are not married yet. I suppose I can chaperone, but I cannot be gone for an entire season. Isobel will be having her child soon."

"Did he mention anything about our wedding?" Cait asked.

The guard glanced to the laird and then shook his head. "No Miss, he did not."

Lacy Mariel huffed and shook her head. "Someone must go fetch him immediately. Did he fall and bump his head?"

Cait let out a long breath. "When ye return please tell him I will not travel and live there without being married first. Perhaps it is best that we pretend the engagement never happened." She took the pin Stuart had given her and held it out to the guard. "Please give him this."

"Oh dear," Lady Mariel said turning to look in the direction of the laird. "Cait, ye should reconsider."

She met the caring woman's gaze. "What would ye do in my place? He asks that I come there and does not mention coming back to marry me. Tell me honestly."

Lady Mariel sighed. A look of resignation on her face. "Exactly what ye are doing."

"I only ask that ye allow me some time to see about my family before we leave."

"Do not be ridiculous. We will discuss the situation and decide what is best. I am disappointed in Stuart and unsure what he is thinking."

In front of the hearth, Catriona and Isobel sat with the

children. Isobel was expecting her first child and spent a great deal of time with Catriona's children. Darach was insistent that she remain close. Not wishing to upset him, she spent most days at the keep. Although, she did escape every so often to the village or to visit Beatrice.

Both women looked up when Lady Mariel approached with Cait in tow. "Stuart is not coming. He sent a message asking that Cait go there instead. Of course, if she went, I would have to go as well."

Isobel's eyes widened. "Ye cannot. I do not wish to be alone until Mother comes."

"Of course, we said no," Lady Mariel replied with a frown. "Honestly, I do not know what has gotten into him. Whoever goes, whether Caelan or Gideon, will have a stern message from me."

"I am sure there is much to do there. Ewan told me the land was overgrown and the locals are reluctant to help. There is the matter of village constable…"

"Ye know more than I do," Cait interrupted Lady Mariel. "I have no idea what is happening. His letters are short only details of the house, rarely of anything else."

Isobel held out her hand. "Cait, there will be a wedding. Ye will remain here with us."

"I do not wish to hold him to his word if he has changed his mind," Cait replied with conviction and then lowered her voice in hopes her mother was not within earshot. "I ask that ye help me secure a position somewhere else. I cannot remain here."

Catriona smiled widely. "If it comes to be that ye need a position—which I hope it doesn't—then ye can be a governess to my bairns. I am already expecting a third."

Relief flooded her and Cait could not help it. Tears overflowed and she sniffed loudly. "Thank ye so much. All of ye have been so very kind to me and my family."

The men must have noticed her crying because Ewan came to them. "Is something wrong?"

His mother gave him a patient look. "Nothing is wrong. We are reassuring Cait that even if there is no wedding, she will have a place with our clan."

"Why will there not be a wedding?" Ewan gawked at Cait. "What happened?"

Lady Mariel pulled him away to explain about the message, and about Cait returning Stuart's crest. Cait took advantage, taking out a handkerchief to wipe her eyes.

Isobel reached for her hand. "Let us wait until after whoever goes returns before we make any permanent changes. I am hopeful Stuart will see reason after receiving yer message."

Cait wasn't so sure. Despite the fact she'd fallen in love with Stuart, resentment was taking up a bigger and bigger space in her heart.

# CHAPTER FIFTEEN

When Stuart and several guards returned to the village, the constable was prepared for a confrontation. Not only had he not left the house, but he'd barricaded himself and hired men to defend him.

Stuart rode up and without hesitation he dismounted and walked closer. The men seemed confused by the cavalier fashion with which he approached the door.

"We cannot allow ye to pass, sir."

He scanned their faces. "Are ye Clan Ross?"

"Aye," one replied for them. "Three of us are."

"I am Stuart Ross, the laird's brother, move aside."

The men's eyes rounded. "We were not told it was ye who we were to defend against." The men allowed him to pass, and he went to the door. He lifted a rock and pounded on it.

The constable no doubt thought it was his guards because he opened the door and then stumbled backward. "Ye were supposed to stop him," he yelled at the men he'd hired.

"Ye did not tell us it was our laird's brother who ye wished to stop," one man replied.

"Pay us and we will go," another said.

The constable's eyes narrowed. Despite being in a dire situation, he still managed to be defiant. "I will not. Ye did nothing for me."

Two of the hired men brushed past Stuart and took the hapless man by the arms holding him up off the ground.

They turned him upside down and shook him until coins fell from his purse. Then when more didn't spill, a third took his dirk and cut the strings so that the purse fell into his palm.

"It should be enough," he informed the others.

"That is more than ye asked," the constable screamed, his face turning a dark red. "Put me down at once."

They dropped him and he hit the floor with a loud thump.

Stuart motioned to his men to take the constable, and they dragged him kicking and screaming out the front door and threw him onto the back of a cart.

Women rushed somewhere in the back. One, who he assumed was the constable's wife screeched loudly. "Get out of my house at once."

"This is my house," Stuart told her calmly as two other women came to stand next to her. "I gave ye plenty of time to leave. My patience is gone. It is ye who must leave at once."

It took about an hour for the women to pile all they could into the back of a wagon, all the while glaring in Stuart's direction. Finally, the constable and his wife climbed into a coach and followed the wagon out of the village.

"Where do ye suppose they are going?" Dougal asked. "It is all Ross lands."

"There is a corner in the southern portion of the island that is claimed by a different clan. I will wager that is where he is headed."

He'd hired a husband and wife from the village to clean the house and ensure the property was prepared for someone to move in.

Once Cait arrived, which he guessed would be in a day or two, he would be able to show her both houses.

UPON RETURNING HOME, Stuart was surprised to note that the guards who'd gone to Keep Ross were already back. He rushed to dismount and hurried into the house, finding the men in the kitchen.

The two exchanged looks, seeming nervous.

"What happened?" Stuart asked when one stood. "Is something wrong with Cait? Mother?"

"No," the man said and again glanced to the other.

For a moment he misunderstood. "When will they come? Did they say?"

"Laird Darach wishes me to inform ye that Lady Isobel is about to give birth and requires yer mother to remain there."

It made sense; he'd not considered it. It would have been nice to see both his mother and Cait's reaction to the house. He was proud of how much had been accomplished not only to the structure, but the lands surrounding it. There were several smaller houses built for the guards. His cousin and wife's home was quite nice as well.

"When will Cait arrive?" he asked while scanning the room and taking in the well-made furnishings.

The guard cleared his throat. "She will not be coming either." The guard held out his hand, in his palm was the Ross crest.

At first, he wasn't sure why she'd sent it. "What did she say exactly?"

"She would not travel here unless married first and she releases ye of yer promise of marriage."

The words sunk in. One by one. Stuart stood frozen to the spot. He noted Maisie and Grace, who'd come out with bowls of food, exchange worried looks. Yet he could not force a word, a breath, or even a movement from his body. It was as if the air was taken, and an invisible force tightened around him.

"Ye have been gone a long while Mister Stuart," Maisie said nearing. When she placed a hand on his shoulder, the spell was broken, and he inhaled sharply.

The men seeming to understand he needed privacy, picked up their bowls of food and left quickly out the back door.

"She said yes," he murmured, unsure what to think. He'd ensured everything was perfect, had spent every waking moment considering how she'd react to what he did to their home.

"This was all for her."

"Was it?" Caelan entered the room.

"I did not know ye were here," Stuart said meeting his half brother's gaze. "Why did ye come?"

Caelan looked to the women and they left the room as well. "I came because someone has to speak to ye and find out what is truly happening."

"What do ye mean?" Stuart blew out a harsh breath. "I asked the woman I love to marry me. I came here to prepare a beautiful home. She repays me by breaking our betrothal. Ye should be asking her not me." He stalked out of the room to the adjoining one to search for the whisky.

Once again, he was of no use to anyone. A man with no purpose.

He poured whiskey into a cup, not bothering to offer Caelan any.

"Stuart," Caelan began. "Ye have been gone for months. Ye could have returned to spend time with the lass. She barely knows ye."

He gulped down the whisky, choking on the fiery contents. After coughing until he lost his breath, Stuart swung in a circle, arms extended. "Everything. The house. The lands. Even the village needed my attention. I had no time—"

"Ye could have sent word and asked for help. If ye would have returned to the keep to Cait and returned with twenty or more men, the work would have been completed sooner."

Fury filled him. "This is *my* home, *my* land," he yelled. "It was up to me to work and complete what needed to be done."

Caelan was silent. Waiting for him to calm.

Stuart could not. He wanted to hit something, to run out the door and keep going until his body gave out.

"Return with me and fix things," Caelan said in a firm tone. "Ye should not have stayed away so long."

Had his brother not heard anything he'd just explained. Even then, the villagers were to gather for him to speak to them the following day. He let out a grunt. "I cannot until after meeting with the villagers tomorrow."

"We will leave right after," Caelan snapped. "Why are ye reluctant? If ye do not care to marry her, then ye must tell her in person. It is the right thing to do." His brother stepped closer. "If not honorable, at least be a man."

His hands curled into fists, but he would not hit his brother. "I have planned to marry her and still will. Obviously, all I did to prepare for her arrival is not enough."

"How was she to know? There is no excuse, Stuart." Caelan's head tilted a bit to the left, a sign he was serious. "No excuse."

There was no use arguing. If someone had been there day to day, they would understand all he did. It seemed that unless actions were done by either Darach, Ewan, or Duncan, it was of little importance.

"No one cares what I do," he finally said falling into a chair. "I give up." He bent putting his head into his hands. "What does it matter?"

"I do not know what this place looked like before, but I can tell ye that it is beautiful now. We are aware that ye have worked tirelessly Stuart. However, ye also had an obligation to yer betrothed. Ye should be committed equally to her."

A long silence stretched between them as Stuart considered his brother's words. Caelan was correct. He'd been gone much too long. Winter was settling in and with it the rainy weather, which would make traveling difficult. Despite the fact he wanted to see Cait, he could not ignore the fact that he was needed at the village.

"We shall travel to the keep, tomorrow. I must see about the villagers. If I do not appear, they will see it as another slight by the Ross family."

His brother nodded in understanding. "I will go with ye."

They ate a robust meal of wild boar that Stuart had recently killed. They'd not eaten any of the livestock yet, as they waited to give the animals time to breed. Once offspring came, then they could slaughter some for meals. For the time being, they ate what either he or the others killed for meat, along with goat's milk and eggs from the chickens. Wheat was acquired from the miller in the village, and the cooks made very good butter.

Stuart watched as Caelan ate. "How is Cait getting along with the family?"

"Yer mother and Isobel have taken her under their wing and have taught her many things. She is being tutored and learning to read and write."

It was hard to imagine the sweet lass being any different. He loved her purity and the delight she took in simple things. "What about her role in the household?"

"As ye are aware, I do not live at the keep," Caelan replied. "But from what I see when I visit, she seems to be doing well. She looks quite different. I suppose it is the new clothing and hairstyle. She seems a bit shy, but that is not surprising."

He could not imagine her being changed at all. Clothes and hair did not totally change a person's appearance, but perhaps the perception from others. "I am glad to hear she is well."

After Caelan went to his bedchamber, Stuart remained awake and went outside to look up at the sky. There was a smell in the air as if it were going to rain. It rained frequently. He prayed for a pair of dry days for the trip back to Ross keep.

But before he left, he would speak to any villagers who gathered tomorrow and ensure they understood that whoever he appointed as constable, would not take advantage of them. Looking toward the guard's houses, he considered if perhaps it would be a good job for Artair or Dougal.

AFTER A SIMPLE meal the next morning, Stuart, Caelan, Artair, and four guardsmen headed to the village. Dougal had left early and gone hunting.

From atop a hill, the village came into view. The quaint

seaside community was pretty to look upon, the smattering of homes and shops welcoming a weary traveler.

Upon their arrival, children raced out into the street running alongside them yelling, "Laird! Laird!"

"Have ye told them ye are not the laird?" Caelan asked.

"I have. But with yer light hair, they must think *ye* to be Darach," Stuart replied with a grin. "Toss them coins."

Caelan's eyes narrowed as he pulled out his purse. He counted out the coins. "One each," he yelled tossing the shimmering bits to the delighted children.

Stuart pulled his horse to a stop and dismounted. A few feet from him, two boys grappled over a coin. He walked to them and taking them by the back of their tunics yanked them off the ground. "Who has a coin?"

The smaller of the two pointed a dirty finger at the other. "He has two, Laird."

"I am not yer laird," he said, but the boys didn't listen as one tried to kick the other.

"Give me my coin," the smaller boy demanded and swung his fist, missing the other boy, but connecting with Stuart's chin.

Both boy's eyes rounded. "Sorry, Laird."

He lowered them to the ground and pointed at the larger one. "Give him back his coin."

After a short standoff, the boy tore his gaze from Stuart and finally produced the coin. He held it out to the younger boy. "Here. But it is mine. I found it first."

Stuart wasn't sure what to say at this juncture. Instead, he pulled out his coin purse and plucked a coin out. He then held it out to the smaller boy, who snatched it.

"Why does he get two?" the larger boy whined. "He does

not deserve it."

"Do ye think to deserve it?" Stuart asked.

When the boy nodded, he asked, "What did ye do to deserve it?"

The larger boy met Stuart's gaze and without blinking blurted, "I am faster, braver, and bigger. One day I will protect ye, Laird. It would behoove ye to have my allegiance."

"Good to know who I should keep an eye out for. A brave man does not attack those smaller than them." Stuart met the boy's gaze. "Brave men learn to be kind."

The boy nodded and hurried to catch up with the smaller one. "Come on. I will ensure no one takes yer coins."

When he walked to the village square, Caelan stood in the center of the small crowd that had gathered. Stuart watched with envy how his brother fended off questions with the experience he'd garnered from his time at Darach's side. So many times, Darach had asked Stuart to sit with him, and he'd declined. Now, he wished to have the knowledge of how to ensure to please the majority.

The villagers seemed reluctant to believe him when Stuart announced there would be a fairer constable. He motioned Artair forward. "This is my cousin, Artair, he will fill the position for now."

The muttering indicated their lack of belief. However, Artair didn't see it as a bad thing. He held up a hand and waited for the people to quiet.

"I propose we get to know one another before ye judge me," his cousin called out. "I will remain here until it is decided if there is anyone better suited for the position."

The people were not totally convinced, but they seemed somewhat appeased when Artair stated his plans to be there at the village square each morning to hear grievances.

After a pair of hours passed and they were convinced Artair was not in danger, Stuart decided it was safe to leave. He ordered the guards to remain as he and Caelan rode away.

"I do hope he decides to remain," Stuart said. "If he doesn't, I will ask Dougal."

"I was going to ask about Dougal. He and Bree may be a better choice," Caelan stated. "As a married couple, they can help with situations that affect both men and women. In addition, Bree is easy to trust and very kind."

"I had thought of it, but then considered she'd make a good friend for Cait."

"They can still be friends. The village is not that far."

As they rode, Stuart looked up to the sky. It was a clear blue, not one cloud to be seen. "I think we will be blessed with good riding weather."

WHEN THE ROSS keep came to view it was evening, and the sun was low on the horizon. They'd ridden at a leisurely pace allowing the horses to rest and drink from a loch.

Stuart's heartbeat quickened at knowing that within moments he'd be seeing Cait again and he could barely keep from urging the horse to a gallop.

"What are ye going to say to her?" Caelan asked casually.

"I am not sure," Stuart replied honestly. "I hope that words will come to me upon seeing her."

Caelan shrugged. "I do not expect that will work out well."

Stuart gave his brother a droll look.

# CHAPTER SIXTEEN

CAIT STRAIGHTENED IN her chair, looking up from her lesson. Her back ached from working on her letters for so long. Still, Isobel seemed intent on continuing.

"Ye should consider resting. The babe should be arriving any day," Cait said hoping her friend would agree.

Instead, Isobel peered over her shoulder. "I must say. I am very impressed with yer penmanship." She then walked to the fireplace and from there to the window. "Write the following . . . Oh, dear, who's that coming?"

Cait began writing and upon completing the sentence looked to Isobel, who remained at the window. "I cannot believe it. Finally, he comes."

Once again Cait bent over her parchment and wrote the words. "That is most curious," she murmured. "I am not sure to have written it correctly. Can ye look?"

When Isobel didn't move and her eyes widened, Cait became concerned. "Are ye feeling pains?"

"I think ye need to see this." Isobel waved her over and Cait got up her stomach sinking at the idea of something dreadful outside.

Two riders approached from the north. One was familiar. It was easy to recognize Caelan, with his style of dress. The other rider, however, was not familiar to her. He wore long hair, and his face was obscured by a beard.

"I wonder why Caelan returned so soon?" Cait said her breath catching. "Do ye expect he brings bad news?"

By Isobel's incredulous look, she missed something. Cait looked from Isobel back outside, but the men had disappeared into the courtyard.

"We should go see what has happened," Cait said. "What is wrong?"

"The man who travels with Caelan, did ye not find him familiar?"

Cait shook her head looking back out despite knowing the men would not be visible. "No. Why?"

Slowly the identity of who the man could be inched into her mind. "Do ye think that was Stuart?"

"Who else could it be?" Isobel asked and then motioned for Cait to follow. "Come let's find out."

"No." Cait looked wildly toward the doorway. "I do not wish to speak to him. I am not prepared."

There was understanding in Isobel's gaze. "I suppose it is best to wait for him to come to ye."

"No." Cait dashed from the parlor. Then realizing she'd have to go through the great room to get to the stairs or out to the kitchen, she turned in a full circle confused and panicked. Finally, she dashed into a small room at the end of the hall and sat on a bed. In the darkness, she felt better, safer.

It wasn't much later that she heard Isobel explaining to someone that she was just there and had walked out. Cait held her breath until finally whoever they were walked away.

The longer she waited the more anxious she became until soon she was crying and could not bring herself to stop. Was it really Stuart? Had he finally returned?

It was time for her to accept her fate and allow things to progress the way they should. As if a massive boulder had been placed on her chest, she could not take full breaths.

There was a soft knock and she inhaled deeply. Cait remained quiet, not wanting to let them know she was in there.

The door opened slowly to show Lady Mariel holding a candlestick. The woman slipped inside and closed the door. "Ye have everyone frantic searching for ye. Guards have been sent to the cottage to see if ye went there."

"Is it Stuart?" Cait whispered.

"Aye, it is," Lady Mariel replied. "I take it ye do not wish to see him at the moment?"

"I am not prepared," Cait replied. "I cannot."

"Very well. Remain here I will reassure everyone ye are unharmed and insist he does not seek ye out until tomorrow at the soonest." Lady Mariel pressed a kiss to Cait's brow. "All will be well. Do not fret dear." She placed the candlestick on a small table and walked out.

A long time later, the door opened, and once again Cait started. This time it was Cora with a tray of food. She placed the tray on the same table and pushed it closer to Cait. Then Cora lowered to a chair and watched her.

"He is unhappy."

Cait lifted a piece of bread and bit off a small piece. "Why?"

"It seems he is upset that ye will not see him."

"I cannot. I am scared he will confirm my fears and will let me go," Cait admitted.

Cora nodded. "He looks so different. Like a wild man."

"Where is he now?"

"In the study with the laird and Mister Caelan."

The study was down the hall. Cait would have to pass it to get to the stairs. "How can I get to my bedchamber?"

"Lady Mariel is going to wait for him to go to bed and fetch ye. However, she did say if he does not, then ye can sleep in here," Cora said in a normal tone.

"Lower yer voice," Cait admonished, her eyes flying to the door.

Cora blew out a breath and whispered. "I would be nervous to see him after so long as well, if I were in yer shoes."

It seemed an eternity before Lady Mariel finally sent for her. She and Cora hurried up the stairs and then to the room she now inhabited. It was at the opposite end of the corridor from Stuart's room.

With the door closed and the key in the lock, finally Cait let out a breath. Cora had tried to stay with her, but Cait had sent her away to find her mother.

"Please tell my mother I will speak with her in the morning. And assure her I am well, just a bit confused."

Cait just couldn't talk to anyone, needing to be alone. What she wanted to do was think about how exactly she'd react to seeing Stuart face-to-face the next day. What would she say to him?

She undressed, washed up at the basin, and donned a clean nightgown. Once that was done, Cait brushed out her hair and braided it. Then she slipped between the blankets. It was a long time before she was able to fall asleep.

LOUD VOICES WOKE her with a start. It was clearly Stuart who spoke. "Tell me where she is Mother."

Lady Mariel's voice was stern. "She will see ye today. Go downstairs for first meal. I will speak to her and ensure she meets with ye."

"Meets?" Stuart said in a tone that sounded furious. "She is my betrothed. I demand to speak to her right now."

There was silence. Then a grunt and retreating footsteps.

Cait opened the door slowly to find an angry Lady Mariel glaring in the direction of the stairwell. "I do not think to have ever seen him so angry."

"I do apologize for the distress this is causing ye. I will dress and speak with him immediately."

Lady Mariel's smile was soft. "I believe it is best that ye should speak to one another. I admit to being worried about Stuart's reaction if ye do not marry him. He is not as strong as he seems dear."

When Lady Mariel walked away, as if magically conjured, Cora appeared. She helped Cait pick out a gown. She chose a simple blue dress that suited her complexion. Once dressed, she ran a brush through her long hair, then twisted the strands together and pinned them at the nape of her neck allowing small whisps to escape around her face. Once that was complete, she let out a breath and walked out of her bedchamber.

With every step toward the parlor, her heart thundered harder and harder. To her surprise, Stuart was not waiting for her. She sent Cora to tell him to meet her there.

At first, she sat in an overstuffed chair. Then too restless, she went to the window. Feeling somewhat as if posing, she went to a different chair and sat. Her lesson from the day before was at the table in front of her and she looked down at the blurry words.

In the time Stuart had been gone, she'd learned to read and write. She'd been taught embroidery and had learned to run a household. In a way, she owed Stuart for providing her with a new life and a better way to support her small family.

Suddenly he was there.

The man she loved walked into the parlor and upon seeing her stopped. His gaze locked with hers and Cait felt as if an invisible force pulled her to him. It took all her willpower not to stand and run into his arms.

What stopped her was that he'd not made the short trip to come see her in months. He'd been gone long enough that she had to stare at him, take in his eyes, lips, and newly shaved chin to recall how he looked.

Stuart also studied her. She'd changed, Cait was aware. Her nails were clean now, her hair shiny, and her clothing of a much better quality. She sat erect, with hands folded on her lap, legs crossed at the ankle.

"Cait. I hoped to see ye upon arriving," he finally said. "Why would ye not see me?"

The question took her by surprise. Did he really not know how much he'd hurt her?

"I was unprepared," Cait finally replied. "For ye to appear so suddenly after so long. I was not sure how to react."

He walked closer and she held her breath until he stopped just a step away. When she looked up, he was frowning. "Ye no longer care for me do ye?"

The conversation was not going as she'd expected. He acted vulnerable, as if he were the injured party.

Cait stood and took a couple of steps backward. "It is ye who showed yer lack of caring by not returning to marry me. It was loud and clear to me that ye hoped by remaining away our betrothal would end."

"That is utter nonsense."

She looked up into his eyes. "Why did ye return? Did Caelan have to convince ye to come and see me?"

When he looked away for a scant moment Cait knew the answer. He did not plan to return.

He reached for her, but when she leaned away he lowered his hand. "I care for ye a great deal Cait and was going to return for ye..."

"When?" Cait interrupted and managed to hitch her chin up to show strength while inside she was dying.

"As soon as everything was ready. I wished the house, the lands... everything to be completed so that when ye came to live there, I could ensure a good home for us."

It was the hardest thing she'd ever done. To look at the man she loved and try to fathom that his feelings had changed.

"I understand that over time, what ye felt for me has diminished. That is why I released ye of yer offer. Do not allow yer brothers to force ye to do something ye do not wish. I will be well."

"Cait. I want to marry ye. I feel the same for ye. Believe me." He reached out and took her hand, then lifted it to his mouth and pressed a kiss to the back of it. "I wish to marry ye."

He seemed so sincere. Everyone insisted he cared for her, but she had a hard time believing it. Perhaps it was her own insecurities. And yet, he had hurt her by not returning even for a short visit.

"My feelings for ye remain, however, understand that I need time." She snatched her hand away. "Please."

Letting out a breath, his gaze locked with hers. "I will try." He motioned to the door, his face softer. "We should go and break our fast."

The last thing she wanted right then, was to eat, but she nodded and allowed him to guide her out. When his hand brushed her elbow, it was as if a bolt of lightning traveled through her body. Her feelings for Stuart had not diminished in the least.

The conversation in the dining room ceased when they walked in. Thankfully, there were only four people sitting around the table. The laird, Isobel, Lady Mariel, and Gideon.

Her mother refused to eat with the laird's family, preferring to take her meals with Cora and Greer in the small room beside the kitchen.

After a beat, Lady Mariel began speaking once again about what would be required for Isobel's delivery. Apparently, Isobel's mother, Lady Macdonald, was traveling there and would arrive in the next day or two.

Stuart held out a chair for her and Cait lowered to sit next to Isobel and across from Lady Mariel.

"How fare ye, Stuart?" Isobel asked. "I did not get an opportunity to speak to ye last night."

"Well," he replied leaning closer to Cait to speak to his sister-in-law. "The bairn is to arrive soon I see."

"Aye, but hopefully not until after the wedding."

It was obvious Isobel was goading Stuart, however, it was Cait who could not keep her eyes from rounding. She looked everywhere except at him.

"I am hopeful that we can marry soon so that Cait can return with me to my lands and see all that I have done for her."

Lady Mariel met Cait's gaze before looking to her son. "I remember the houses there. The one in the village is lovely, but the one away from there is larger and better suited for a family, I believe."

"Two houses?" Cait asked. "Why are there two houses?"

It was Stuart who replied. "Our great uncle preferred to live in the village, so he had a house built there. Our grandfather lived in the larger one outside the village."

Lady Mariel nodded. "My husband's father passed away a long time ago, so the house has remained empty for many years." She looked at Stuart. "Does someone live in the one in the village?"

"A constable, who'd been given free rein for too long, lived there. He was cruel to the villagers, demanding taxes and doling out punishment. Artair is there now, as acting constable, until I can find someone who wishes to perform the task."

"Why don't ye do it? The lands are yers, the villagers yer responsibility. Ye are the area laird, Stuart," Darach said. "The people there need help and encouragement. The village is quite large is it not?"

"Aye," Stuart replied. "I would say about one hundred or so."

Turning to Cait, Stuart looked at her. "I will let Cait decide where we live. Ye may prefer to be closer to the village or may find the country house with the larger gardens and livestock more to yer liking."

Every eye on her, Cait felt trapped.

"I suppose it depends on how things go."

"I want to marry ye. I feel the same for ye as when I left."

"Then why did ye stay away?"

"I was preparing things for ye."

"Did ye not consider I wanted to be part of that instead of sitting here waiting?"

His eyes narrowed and nostrils flared. "And ye do not care that I have fought so hard every day to ensure the house would be a place I would be proud to bring ye to?"

Cait huffed. "Ye could have come sooner."

"Ye could have traveled there when my brothers came to visit."

At a standoff, they kept eye contact, neither giving ground. Finally, Stuart stood and looked down at her. "Ye should not have to fight so hard to break our betrothal. I accept. It is broken."

He stormed from the room leaving her surrounded by stunned people unsure of what to say.

Finally, Cait let out a breath she'd been holding.

"I will speak to him," Darach said, then looked to Cait. "Are ye hurt? Or do ye not love my brother any longer? Because I will assure ye, Stuart continues to love ye dearly. He is heartbroken."

"It is partly my fault. Perhaps I still cannot believe someone like him loves me?" Cait replied, wishing she could disappear.

The laird stood and walked out after his brother.

"I am not sure what to do." Cait's whisper was met with a long silence.

Isobel covered her hand with hers. "I do believe the best thing is for ye to give Stuart some time to calm."

"Do ye love him?" Lady Mariel asked.

"I do," Cait admitted noting that Gideon had not stopped eating and was oblivious to the conversation.

"Then ye should tell him. One of ye has to put pride aside if ye wish to have a life together."

Cait walked out of the dining room unsure of where to go. A part of her needed to be outdoors, another urged her to hide in her bedchamber and cry.

She chose to go outside.

# CHAPTER SEVENTEEN

STUART PACED ACROSS the front of the stables. The crisp air helped to cool his temperament, but only a bit. He was too angry to do much more than continue walking back and forth, the dirt crushing under his leather boots.

Darach appeared from the house and Stuart braced himself for whatever lecture was forthcoming. He began to wish not to have come at all. He should have accepted that Cait no longer wished to marry him.

His brother's purposeful steps made short work of the courtyard. When close enough to speak, Darach's expression was warm. "It hurts me when ye or any of our brothers hurt. I wish I could take it away."

If not for being outdoors, Stuart would have embraced his brother tightly. Instead, he swallowed past the huge lump in his throat the words had brought. "Thank ye, Darach. I suppose ye have to learn that every one of us will have to traverse both hills and valleys."

"I am not prepared for being a father," Darach admitted. "If what I feel for ye, Ewan, Gideon, Duncan, Ella, and even Calean is any indication, I will surely go mad."

"Ye will be an extraordinary father to the wee bairn."

"Cait loves ye Stuart," Darach said. "However, she is hurt, and it makes her reluctant to give in."

"I love yer as well. I do not have any idea what to do."

"Do not flee. If ye can learn anything from my experience with Isobel, and Duncan's with Beatrice, know that going away is not the answer right now."

Stuart chuckled without mirth. "Why do we all run away at the most important times in our life?"

"A family trait?" Darach said shaking his head.

"Like both ye and Duncan, I must seek redemption and pray that the woman I love forgives me."

"She will. She loves ye," Darach said turning to the house. "Are ye going back inside?"

"In a moment. I must walk some and clear my head first."

While walking through the trees, Stuart considered how much he missed the familiar landscape. He'd spent his entire life there, traipsing through the forest with his brothers. First, playing games as children then later hunting as men.

There were so many memories scattered throughout the woods and on past at the village. However, it was time to move on and forge his future, but he was glad to be close enough to be able to visit.

He'd been a fool. It was clear to him now that he should have done more than send a missive or message here and there. Instead of assuming, he should have asked Cait what she wished to do. And though he suspected where she'd prefer to live, she should have been part of remodeling the larger home to help make the decision clearer.

It hurt that she barely gave any acknowledgment for all he'd done. Then he realized, she had no idea what he'd been doing apart from what he'd written in his letter. The notes had been short, mostly a small passage about the house, with closing comments about missing her, wishing her well, and an assurance he would return soon. In return, her letters had told him of her days, of missing him and wishing for him to come and see her.

All along, she'd been asking for him to visit, to see him and he'd been too intent on the house and the land. He didn't shoulder all the blame, because she could have come and visited when one of his brothers traveled to his lands. At the same time, she was new to life as a member of the laird's family and probably not used to asserting herself.

A deer appeared and looked at him for a moment before scampering off into the trees. Stuart looked after it and for a moment was a bit jealous of the animal's freedom.

It shook him to realize that he'd been free of any responsibility most of his life and yearned for what he had now. The responsibility of lands, servants, a village, and a wife. Was it possible that he too had to learn to be different?

When arriving at a clearing, he lowered to a fallen tree and closed his eyes. The last time he'd been at that particular spot, he and Cait had been together. It was the day he'd realized beyond a doubt that he loved the pretty lass.

She'd changed so much since he left. No longer meek and trying to fade into the background, the new Cait was a graceful beauty. Upon entering the parlor that morning, he'd almost not recognized her and started to introduce himself. Once he looked closer, his Cait was still there, only now she looked even more stunning than the beauty he'd left behind.

Before he'd left, she'd had a hard time hiding her awareness of him, now she was aloof and distant, and he had no idea what she was thinking.

When she looked at him, her eyes were clear and penetrating, but he could not read her expression because it was guarded. How terrible that he caused her to change in that way.

She admitted to still having feelings for him. There was hope. He would not give up. It could be that he would remain much longer, but no matter what it took, Stuart was determined to gain Cait's full love back.

A horse and rider came upon him and stopped. He immediately recognized Torac, Cait's brother. The warrior dismounted and walked closer. "I was not aware ye had returned," the man said.

"I returned only yesterday," Stuart replied. "Where are ye headed?"

Torac shrugged. "Returning from the village. I went to visit my mother."

The man studied Stuart for a moment. "Are ye and my sister to marry while ye are here?"

"If I can convince her. She broke off our betrothal."

Torac's eyebrows rose. "I was not aware."

"Aye, my fault for staying away so long." Stuart wondered about Torac's opinion of their marriage. "Have ye spoken to her lately?"

Torac shrugged. "Cait and I are not close. Despite her living at the keep, she and I do not spend much time together. It has been less than a year since I met her and my half brother. It is not immediate that one feels a familiar connection."

"I plan to convince her to marry me and regain her trust again. I love Cait. My plan is that she along with her brother and her mother will be leaving to live in the northwest."

Torac's lips curved. "It will be good for her. I am glad."

As Cait's half brother rode away, Stuart felt stronger about his plans to win Cait back.

He stood and looked up to the cloudy sky realizing he needed to head back to the keep before the rain fell. By the darkness of the clouds, a storm was about to hit.

The rain began falling hard as he started the trek back to the keep. He'd not realized how far he'd walked and now regretted not bringing his horse. Especially when it became dark, the rain falling so hard he could barely see.

Finally, he gave up and sought shelter by a grouping of trees that safeguarded him from the downpour. It was a long while before he gave up waiting it out and decided to continue his trek back to the keep. The rain was not relenting, and he could no longer control his shivering from the cold.

Each step was a struggle as he fought the pouring rain and lashing wind that pushed him backward. His foot slipped on the mud, and he tumbled down the side of a small hill, cursing the entire way.

When he came to a stop, flat on his back, he stared up at the darkened sky. The rain continued, ridiculously hard, the drops pelting him like small stones.

By the time he walked out of the forest, he could barely keep upright. It took monumental effort to put one foot in front of the other. He felt foolish that his teeth chattered, and in a way, he felt like a stupid lad for not keeping better track of time, distance, and the weather.

Just as he walked into the house, Cait was crossing from the parlor to the stairs. She stopped and stared at him, taking him in head to toe. "What happened to ye?"

"It's raining," he replied unable to keep the annoyance from his tone. The last person he wished to run into at the moment was the one who'd caused him to walk so far in the first place.

"Go to the kitchen door, Greer will instruct them to pour a hot bath for ye."

She made shooing motions with both hands forcing him to walk back outside and to the kitchen doorway. He burst through the door and into the kitchen. "I-I…n-need a b-bath," he said between chattering teeth.

Greer's wide eyes did the same as Cait, running from his face to the trail of mud he'd created from the doorway. "Of course, dear." She ushered him closer to the hearth, the heat from the fire permeating his freezing wet clothing.

Quickly instructing the servants to fetch water, and a pair of lads to drag the wooden tub to the adjoining room, she then began helping Stuart undress, peeling layer after layer of sopping wet clothing from his shivering form.

A few moments later, he sunk into the warm water and had hot cider warming his belly. The smell of a delicious meal—he hoped to soon be enjoying—was coming from the other room.

He heard Cait speaking in the other room. He didn't respond or pay attention, as it was doubtful she deemed him worthy of her time.

Instead, he stepped from the water and draped a cloth around his midsection. Once that was done, he took a second cloth and began drying his hair, face, and chest.

"Stuart…" Cait had walked in and now stood frozen. Her

gaze locked on his chest. Then slowly it traveled down to the precarious hold the cloth had on his hips. Finally, she dragged her eyes up to meet his.

Then he saw it, the attraction she still had for him.

"Yes?" he replied nonchalantly. "What is it Cait?"

"My brother spoke to me…" She stopped speaking when the towel around his hips slipped a bit. "Uh…he said to have seen ye in the forest."

Afraid the cloth would fall to around his ankles, Stuart gripped the cloth where it joined and pulled it closed tucking the end back into place. The entire time Cait watched not realizing he observed her.

"What did yer brother say?"

"What?" She blinked rapidly. "I should allow ye to dress instead of standing here like a ninny."

Stuart walked closer to her. "Tell me."

Her eyes seemed to glaze over before focusing on his. "My brother?"

He moved closer until barely a breath between them. "Aye. What did ye say?"

"Oh." Her lips parted. "That ye…" She swallowed when he reached up with both hands raking his fingers through his too-long hair. "That ye told him about plans for me, my mother, and my brother…" Again, she stopped mid-sentence when he wet his bottom lip.

"I should allow ye to dress. We can speak later."

Stuart let the corners of his mouth lift just a bit. "Good, I have much to say to ye."

Her eyes widened when his cloth slipped a bit too low, and the patch of hair just above his sex peeked out.

"Goodness." Her eyes rounded as she back out of the room running into the door before turning and escaping.

Stuart chuckled.

"Here are some clean clothes," Greer said in a flat tone.

"Thank ye," Stuart said still smiling.

Greer shook her head. "I do not know what ye did to that poor lass, but her face was red when she flew past me and out of the kitchen."

He shrugged then grinned wickedly at Greer when she rolled her eyes.

Once dressed, Stuart decided to search for Cait. Planning to take advantage of every moment that he could spend with her.

"I heard ye were soaked through." His mother neared automatically feeling his brow. "I pray ye do not become ill."

"I feel much better now that I've had a hot bath. Greer gave me something to drink to dispel any sickness."

In the great room, there were people milling about taking shelter from the hard rain outside. He searched the faces, noting that Cait was not among them.

"Where is Cait?"

His mother gave a one-shouldered shrug. "I do not know. I am caring for Isobel. She is feeling a bit poorly. I suppose either in the parlor or upstairs in the sitting room."

He walked through the great room, stopping twice to speak to people who asked about his new home.

In the parlor, Gideon was with a woman Stuart did not recognize. By the look on his brother's face, he'd interrupted something.

Stuart nodded in acknowledgment. "I am seeking out

Cait."

"She is not here," Gideon replied. Realizing his lack of manners, his brother motioned to the woman. "May I present, Margaret McLeary. This is my brother, Stuart."

The woman bowed her head. "It is nice to meet ye."

Whoever she was, the woman was much older than Gideon; but by the way she looked at his younger brother, they were well acquainted. Gideon had a penchant for getting into trouble with women.

"Is everything well?" Stuart asked.

"Perfectly fine," the woman replied sliding a glance in Gideon's direction.

With a bored expression, Gideon said, "Aye. Miss McLeary was just about to leave."

"I cannot possibly," the woman interjected, motioning to the window. "I must wait for the storm to pass. Sit with me, Gideon."

When Gideon sat, Stuart walked out and went to Darach's study. His brother was pacing but stopped at seeing him.

"Do ye know who the woman is in the parlor with Gideon?" Stuart asked. "I got the feeling she is up to something."

Darach frowned. "I saw her walk past. She is a widow that I believe Gideon has been going off to meet with. When he stopped visiting, she came here."

"Is our brother once again in a quandary?"

"Aye," Darach replied. "She will be disappointed if she tries to force him to do anything."

Feeling better at knowing Gideon was protected, Stuart hurried up the stairs in search of Cait. She was in the sitting room with another woman. She seemed familiar, one of the kitchen maids, if he remembered correctly.

"Mister Stuart." The woman rose and curtsied. "May I fetch something for ye?"

He looked to the sideboard. "No thank ye, I will pour myself a brandy. If ye could please excuse us."

"Of course." The woman turned to Cait and smiled before walking out.

"Cora," Cait said looking at him. "She is my companion now."

He took his time pouring brandy into two small glasses while pondering what to say to her. She was composed now, but her gaze followed him.

"I went to the clearing in the woods."

She tilted her head to the side. "Where?"

"The place where ye and I enjoyed time together. Do ye remember?"

Stuart held out the glass to her and she took it, their hands touching. Cait inhaled sharply.

"I do," she said taking a dainty sip. "Ye should have ridden instead of walking."

"I know that now," he said lowering to sit next to her. "I was angry and needed time to think."

She studied her glass. "I am glad ye returned relatively unscathed."

"I saw a beautiful doe. She reminded me of ye."

It was obvious she didn't know what he'd say next by her questioning look. "How?"

"Innocent, delicate, and beautiful. Looking perfect as she walked through the trees, cautious of anything that crossed her path."

"Our first conversation was out there," Cait said. "Ye were chastising yer horse."

"Aye, I remember." He placed his hand on her forearm. "Cait I cannot express how much I regret hurting ye. Will ye forgive me?"

"I do understand that ye wished to make everything perfect at the house before I came. Yer family has reassured me and explained it. However, I feel as if I was not part of your life while ye were away. Ye have worked hard for a home for us but left me here alone for months. I had no idea what ye were doing."

"There is so much I wish to share with ye." Stuart waited for a moment. "I should have come for ye. I should have visited. I can become so very short sighted when working on something that is important to me."

Turning toward him, she met his gaze. There was something in the way she looked at him that made him want to kiss her, hold her, and reassure her. However, he knew to tread lightly.

Finally, she said. "Tell me about the house and the lands."

# CHAPTER EIGHTEEN

THE GREEN FLECKS in Stuart's eyes had a mesmerizing effect. Cait could not tear her eyes away. She was glad he'd sought her out and wished to spend time with her.

Her brother had told her that Stuart professed to love her and wished to take her back to his lands. Not only her, but he'd mentioned her mother and brother and that meant a great deal.

She wanted to hear everything he had to say. So Cait pushed her doubts away as she waited for him to pour another bit of brandy into their glasses.

"The house is on the side of a hill..." he began and described everything in great detail. From the layout of the house to the two women who worked in the kitchen. He told her of purchasing chickens and other animals so that soon the hills behind the house would be brimming with sheep, the courtyard filled with chickens, and the pens crowded with goats.

"On one side of the house where the morning sun shines, we planted a vegetable garden. On the opposite side, I hope ye will plant flowers." Stuart stopped speaking and placed a kiss on her cheek. "If ye agree to marry me and come to live there that is."

Cait knew she would, but waited, wanting to hear more.

"I hired men to till the large field that we cleared," Stuart continued. "The field is also on the west side of the house, from where we harvested trees to build guard quarters and animal pens. We had to down a lot of trees to repair the house as well."

He took a large drink of brandy. "I am convinced ye will love it."

"I do wish to see it," Cait admitted.

Stuart leaned forward until their lips almost touched. "Return with me."

"The baby," Cora appeared at the door. "The laird's bairn is arriving."

Cait jumped to her feet, both from the news and because Cora walked in on Stuart about to kiss her. She looked to Stuart. "We should go see."

Together they hurried down the corridor to Darach and Isobel's bedchamber on the opposite side of the house.

Stuart stopped outside the door, joining Gideon and Darach. Just then Caelan and Duncan appeared at the top of the stairs. Both were soaked through but grinning.

Cora turned in a circle and held out her arm stopping both men. "I will have baths drawn so ye do not catch yer death."

The brothers nodded and then went to their eldest brother, who looked pale and worried.

Cait walked past the group and into the room.

Isobel was atop the bed, her face contorted with pain. "Where is Mother? Beatrice?" she asked Cait.

"I am sure their travel is delayed because of the storm," Cait replied.

When Isobel began to cry, Lady Mariel and Annis, soothed her.

The midwife looked up at Isobel. "Ye can push now."

Isobel shook her head. "No, I can't," she pronounced emphatically.

"Ye must darling," Lady Mariel said in a soft tone. "Yer mother will arrive shortly and will be so proud of ye and so very happy to see the wee one."

Just then the door burst open, and Beatrice hurried to her sister's bedside. "So sorry Issy. I had to stop and dry myself before coming up here." She patted her sister's stomach. "Come along now ye wee bairn."

Happy to see a member of her family, Isobel began to push. Between pains, they did their best to distract her with silly anecdotes until the pains were so close together, there was no time to do much more than soothe her.

Cait worried one moment and felt pride the next. That women were so brave to go through something so painful to bring a child forth was awe-inspiring.

At the sound of the baby's first wail, everyone began to cry.

"It is a boy," the midwife announced holding up the red-faced child.

Lady Mariel hurried to the foot of the bed. "I will bundle him up." She took the baby and swaddled it, then placed it in Isobel's arms.

Beatrice beamed. "My wee one and yers will grow up together." The sisters hugged, sharing a loving moment that brought more tears.

Annis went to the door to announce the baby's arrival. There were masculine sounds of cheering and laughter.

Once the afterbirth was brought forth and Isobel was settled onto clean bedding, they walked out so that Darach could enter and meet his son.

Before walking out, Cait turned just as Darach knelt beside the bed and pulled both Isobel and the bairn into an embrace. For a moment she hesitated. It was a scene she'd never forget. A loving couple welcoming their firstborn.

Everyone was gathered in the hallway, hugging, and speaking over one another in celebration. Unsure of how to get around them, she moved against the wall to wait.

Stuart hurried over and lifted Cait off her feet, turning in a circle. When he placed her down, his face was bright with happiness. "The heir to the lairdship is born," he said in a hoarse voice.

He kept one arm around her waist as they continued to celebrate.

As one the group went down the stairs together. Beatrice with Duncan, Gideon with his mother, and Stuart beside Cait. At the bottom of the stairs, Gideon called out that the babe was born, and the people gathered cheered.

Wine was poured, and several men began playing music. The room became bright when more candles were lit making the celebration more festive.

Greer and the other cooks hurried out from the kitchen with trays of sweet cakes. Cait noticed that Annis hurried up the stairs with warm cakes and a bowl of soup for Isobel and the laird.

Already feeling a bit lightheaded after the brandy, Cait took small sips of the celebratory wine while enjoying the cheerful conversations surrounding her. For a moment she considered that this would be her family if she and Stuart reconciled.

She smiled brightly when her mother walked close and was asked to sit with them.

"He rarely looks away from ye," her mother said with a soft smile.

Cait turned to her mother. "Are ye happy here? I want ye to be."

"I am happy wherever ye and Brice are," her mother replied. Her mother looked lovely. Having good food and without the lines of worry, she seemed younger and much prettier.

"Perhaps ye will find someone and marry again," Cait said loving it when her mother blushed.

"Cait the things ye say," she admonished.

LULLED BY THE wine and music, soon Cait could barely keep her eyes open. Her mother had gone to bed and both Lady Mariel and Beatrice had gone back to see Isobel.

When she stood, Stuart stood with her. "I will see ye upstairs."

Cait was glad for it. She wanted to be close to him for a bit longer.

They walked up the stairs in silence until reaching her doorway. "Why did ye move here?" Stuart asked. "This is a very small chamber is it not?"

Cait walked into the room. "I find it very comfortable."

When she turned Stuart had walked in behind her, his large body shrinking the room considerably. He looked around. "Much too small."

Cait laughed. "I can see why ye would say that."

Then she was in his arms. She'd be hard-pressed to say

who closed the distance first. They'd move toward each other at almost the same time.

However, it was Stuart who covered her mouth with his and pulled her closer. The kiss so wonderful, tears slid down her cheeks.

When he continued the kiss and tasted her tears, Stuart pulled her against his chest. "Do not cry. I will not kiss ye again, I promise. Allow me to stay with ye for a moment longer."

Cait pushed back a bit and swatted at his chest. "That is not why I cry. I cry because I missed ye so much."

His chest expanded as he took a large breath. "I missed ye too Cait. I love ye and do not wish to ever lose ye."

Looking into his eyes, she knew he was truthful as his own were shiny. "I love ye Stuart. Kiss me again."

The kiss became passionate quickly. She parted her lips for his tongue to push past and raked her fingers through his hair wanting more of him.

When she slipped both hands under his tunic to feel his skin, Stuart's breath caught. Needing no further urging, he pulled it over his head then took her hands and placed them against his chest. "I am yers, Cait."

At first, she was tentative, slowly sliding her palms over the surface of his muscular chest, then to his back. Wherever she touched, Cait could feel his restraint.

"Ye have a beautiful body," Cait whispered.

He cupped her face and lifted it so that he could kiss her as she continued to discover him.

It was not surprising to find that her vest was untied and her top unbuttoned shortly thereafter. Stuart turned her around, and while his lips traveled down the side of her throat, he managed to untie all the bindings of her skirts as well, until they were in a puddle at her feet.

He lifted her into his arms and walked to the bed where he lowered along with her to lay beside her.

His mouth closed over hers. His hand traveling under her chemise, sliding over her skin, sending ripples of awareness to every inch of her body.

While trailing his tongue from her throat to her breasts, Stuart removed his breeches leaving himself completely naked.

Cait lifted her head wanting to see him, but all she could see was his head and shoulders. Curious as to what would happen, she slid her hands down his sides imitating what he did. Stuart lifted his head and smiled at her.

"Marry me, Cait." His hand slid between her legs and she gasped at the awakening tingles.

His fingers delved between her folds touching her in a way that made her take a sharp breath.

"Say ye will," he insisted.

"We should ensure…ah."

He began circling the very core of her sex with his fingertips and she had to grip the bedding in an attempt at control.

"Say yes," he whispered in her ear, as he continued the slow, torturous, movements.

Cait couldn't breathe. She gasped trying to take in more air. Unable to control herself, she lifted her hips urging Stuart to take her to that forbidden place. The one she remembered from their time in the forest clearing.

"I cannot wait. Please…"

"Say ye will marry me," he insisted. "Or I will stop."

"Yes!" she cried out and then dissolved as he pinched her lightly sending her into a fast spin.

Cait grabbed his hips. "More," she urged. "Stuart."

"Are ye sure ye want to take things further?" His Adam's apple bobbed, and his voice caught. "I love ye, Cait. I am willing to wait."

"I do not wish to wait any longer. I am done waiting," Cait replied nodding. "I am very sure."

When he lifted to take himself in hand, she finally saw his sex. It was not what she expected. It was rather appealing. Longer and thicker than his hand, it was flushed and quite hard.

The sight of his arousal made the heat between her legs intensify and she marveled at the sensations. How was it possible for it to happen?

"Do ye feel it too?"

"What do ye feel?" He asked testing her entrance. "Relax, beauty."

She inhaled sharply at the tight fit. "A bit hot down there. Wet."

"Aye, I feel that way as well."

"Take a deep breath," he instructed and when she did, he thrust into her.

Cait cried out into Stuart's mouth. Thankfully it muffled her sound enough that no one would hear. Tears slipped from the corners of her eyes at the sharp pain that began to ebb immediately. "It hurt."

"Only once," Stuart said kissing her tears and beginning to move. He slid out just a bit and then drove back in.

Cait concentrated on each movement, her eyes closed and

her hands on his bottom. She liked the feel of his flexing with each movement and soon was entranced by the rhythm he set. When he kissed her and began moving faster, she had to break the kiss to catch her breath. Something explosive was happening and she wondered if what he did would render her again.

Every muscle in her body tensed as the heat grew hotter. She didn't want to move for fear of dousing the ember that swelled within.

By the time Stuart was pumping into her with vigor, Cait's legs were straight, and she held her breath both fighting and welcoming the wave that threatened.

Suddenly she shuddered with a release so hard, she could not make a sound. She screamed silently, her fingernails digging into Stuart's shoulders. Then slowly everything settled into place.

It was delightful and a bit scary if she was to be honest.

Meanwhile, Stuart seemed to feel the same, he'd lost his rhythm, went rigid, and uttering a deep groan he collapsed over her.

Cait wanted to laugh at how silly they must have looked. But never before in her life had she felt so as one with another human.

Lazily sliding her hands down his back, she grinned at him like a madwoman.

Stuart lifted his head and met her gaze. He didn't look happy, but instead concerned. "Did ye mean it?"

"What are ye referring to?" Cait asked genuinely perplexed.

"That ye will marry me. I want ye to be my wife forever, Cait."

She pressed a kiss to his shoulder. "I said I would. I love ye Stuart and want ye to be my husband forever."

He lowered his head to the pillow beside hers. The man was quite heavy and yet she never wanted him to move.

"Ye love me?"

Her entire being filled with emotion. "More than ye will ever know."

A moment later, he shifted to lay beside her and pulled the bedding over them.

"Ye cannot remain. Someone will see us," Cait whispered.

"We are to be married," Stuart replied with a yawn. "I will sneak out in the morning."

"I cannot wait for ye to see our bedchamber at the house," he said groggily. "It has a very large bed."

His feet probably hung over the end of her small bed. "Are ye comfortable?"

When he pulled her against him and nuzzled her neck, she sighed.

"I am very comfortable." Cait giggled knowing he lied.

# CHAPTER NINETEEN

TWO DAYS LATER, there was a feast to celebrate the laird's firstborn and the arrival of Isobel and Beatrice's mother, Lady Macdonald.

Ella Ross Macdonald, who'd married the new laird Evander Macdonald, came as well.

Cait immediately loved Ella, who claimed that Cait was the most beautiful woman she'd ever met. It was sweet of the other women to agree with her and for their husbands to reassure them that they were the most beautiful in their eyes.

"I for one am glad to be preparing for *this* son's wedding," Lady Mariel announced, and everyone laughed.

"It took a great deal of effort on my part last night to convinced her to marry me," Stuart said, and Cait gasped at what he alluded to. Then she blushed when Stuart kissed her in front of them.

"I want to hear that story," Ella said giving her a saucy wink.

"No!" Cait replied. Then realizing she'd taken the bait; she covered her face with both hands as everyone began laughing again.

"When will the wedding be, dear?" her mother asked and Cait shrugged. "I am leaving the decision to ye and Lady Mariel. Stuart wishes to remain for a few weeks longer. He is spending time with the laird."

"Yer brother and I will be leaving with ye when ye are ready," her mother stated. Then looked over her shoulder. "Oh, there he goes again."

A man walked to stand across the room. With silver at his temples, he was a bit older than her mother. His gaze darted to where they sat.

Cait's eyes rounded, and she looked to her mother. "Who is he?"

"A bother," her mother replied, then snuck a look at the man.

Leaning closer to Stuart, Cait asked him in a whisper who the man was.

Stuart looked over to the man who was now speaking to another. "Lyall Ross. He is my late father's cousin. He moved to the village after his wife died and works here with the livestock. He is good with animals."

His gaze met hers and butterflies fluttered in her stomach. "Why do ye ask?"

"I believe he is interested in my mother."

Stuart smiled. "That is good."

"I am not sure. Mother seems put off."

"Then why does she keep stealing glances in his direction?" Stuart asked with a grin.

"Come with me," Stuart said taking her hand. When the others looked to them, he gave them a lazy smile.

"I am going to speak to Cait about setting a wedding date."

His mother waved a hand in the air. "It will be in a sennight."

"In a sennight," Cait repeated.

"Nonetheless, come with me."

They walked out through the front door and past the gates to the side of the house. From there he guided her to a slight hill and then lowered her to the ground. "Sit with me."

Cait sat next to him looking out to the sea. It was cool outside, but not so cold that it was uncomfortable.

"Do ye wish for me to ask Uncle Lyall to come with us?" Stuart asked. "If he is hoping to court yer mother, it would be useful if they were near one another."

It was the sweetest offer and Cait cupped his jaw with her hand. "Ye are so kind to offer. I am not sure. She protests, but ye are right, she does seem very interested. Perhaps it would be a good idea. However, we must not let her know it was just now planned."

"Very well," Stuart replied. He looked into the distance. "I need to return to my lands."

Cait stiffened. "Before the wedding?"

When his eyes widened, Cait wanted to slap him. "Nay, it can wait, I'm worried about Artair."

"If ye cannot wait until we are married, then if ye go, I will go with ye."

Thinking on how very much he loved her. "I'll send Gideon," Stuart said and pulled her against his chest. "Can I come to yer chamber tonight?"

"No."

He blew out a breath. "Ye are going to make me wait to be married?"

"Aye, I am. We should have not done it. We are not married yet." Despite her stern reply, she hid how much she wished he would insist and perhaps even come to her chamber without permission. But she knew he wouldn't, and she couldn't bring herself to say yes.

"Then I will have to kiss ye until ye melt into my arms."

"That happens every time," Cait said lifting her face so that he would kiss her.

THE DAYS PASSED quickly. Soon the keep was overflowing with people who'd come to attend the wedding of the laird's brother.

With each passing day, Cait had become more nervous. It was late morning the day before the wedding and she sat in the small room next to the kitchen with her mother and Greer going over the meal that would be served.

"It is a wonderful menu," her mother exclaimed with excitement. "Two boars, pheasants, and fish, then the sweet cakes and stews. I can hardly wait."

Cait smiled despite the persistent tightness in her stomach. "I am so nervous; my stomach has been in knots. I've not been able to eat the last two days without feeling sick."

Tapping her hand, Greer smile. "Do not be nervous, all will be fine. Ye will be a beautiful bride to a very handsome man. I know ye look forward to time alone with him, but remember, once the wedding is over, ye will have a lot of work to do. Be sure ye learn as much as ye can before leaving."

"I have," Cait replied. "Lady Mariel has ensured I am well versed in running a household."

"I am so very happy for ye," Cora said walking in. "I cannot wait to help ye run the new house."

Cait smiled when a plate of food was slid in front of her by Cora.

"If ye eat here in peace, without all the discussion of weddings and the presence of the man ye are to marry, then the food will settle much better."

She ate everything on the plate and then drank cider while her mother, Cora, and Greer also ate. It was refreshing to have a chat with the women she most trusted and loved. She would miss Greer greatly and made the woman promise to come visit. Both Greer and her daughter, Finella, became excited at the prospect.

When she walked out, her mother followed. "Cait, I must tell ye something."

At her mother's serious expression, Cait hesitated. "Is something wrong Mother?"

"The man, Lyall informed me that yer husband-to-be offered to move him to yer new home. Did ye know anything about it?"

It was hard not to laugh at her mother's pointed look. "I did not ask Stuart to invite him if that is what ye are asking." It was not a lie, so she didn't feel bad about the statement.

"Very odd," her mother said. "He is quite happy about it. Did ye know he is a Ross?"

"Mother, I had not noticed the man until the other day when ye pointed him out to me." Again, she was not lying "Does it bother ye that he is to go live where we are?"

"I suppose not. It has nothing to do with me, so," her mother said with a shrug. "I just think it odd that he is to come. He'd not mentioned it before."

"So ye have conversations with him then?" Cait asked

innocently. She'd seen her mother speaking to Lyall several times. Each time, she'd acted put out, but her cheeks had pinkened.

"Not so much a conversation." Her mother pushed at Cait's arm. "Go see about yer intended and stop asking so many questions."

When Cait went to her bedchamber all of her items had been removed. She hurried back out and to the sitting room, but it was empty.

Deciding to question Stuart she knocked on his door, but no one answered. She pushed the door open and peered in. A few familiar things had been placed in the bedchamber, so she went inside and began sorting through them.

"Oh, there ye are," Cora exclaimed with a smile. "Lady Mariel asked that I move yer personal effects in here."

"What about tonight?" Cait asked. "I will have to sleep elsewhere, and I require some of these items."

"Oh, goodness," Cora said rushing to her side. "In my excitement, I totally forgot about tonight." She giggled and went to a wardrobe and extracted a night rail.

"Where is my wedding dress?" Cait asked as they walked back out and toward her own room.

"Lady Mariel said ye will dress in the sitting room. She has it now and will bring all of yer items to the sitting room after last meal."

Cait shook her head. "I am not used to any of this. I wonder what other things are planned that I do not know about yet."

"Cait," Lady Mariel said coming from the direction of the sitting room. "Isobel wants to see ye. Also, ye will not go down for last meal nor will ye see Stuart at all until the wedding. Ye will take yer meals in the sitting room."

She eyed the items both she and Cora carried. "Come along, bring it all with ye."

They followed Lady Mariel to a small room adjoining hers. "Now this is perfect. Stuart will not find ye here."

Once she put all her items down, Cait then went back out to see Isobel. She was anxious to see the wee bairn.

The laird's bedchamber was warm. There was a cheery fire in the hearth and the curtains were drawn to hold the warmth in.

Isobel sat up in the bed and was drinking from a cup when Cait walked in. Her face brightened at seeing her.

"I am so happy about yer wedding. I wish I could be there."

Lady Macdonald, who sat in a chair in the corner with the sleeping child in her arms, gave Isobel a pointed look. "The bairn was quite big and ye have to heal properly before traipsing about."

"It is just downstairs and Darach offered to carry me," Isobel protested and then looked at Cait with a warm smile. "I have a gift for ye."

Cait smiled and walked nearer. "Ye are much too kind."

"It is something I think ye will like to have." Isobel motioned to a bundle on a table beside the bed.

Feeling giddy, Cait lifted it and looked at it for a long time. "This is my first gift."

"Ye will get more tomorrow. But I am happy to give ye yer first wedding gift." Isobel grinned.

"What I mean is that this is my first gift ever. I have never received a gift before."

"Not even from yer father or mother?" Lady Macdonald exclaimed. "How sad."

Isobel gave her mother a patient look. "Not everyone has the means for frivolity. All money has to be saved for necessities."

"Oh dear, that was thoughtless of me," Lady Macdonald exclaimed, but then brightened. "Open it."

Rolled neatly inside the parchment was a beautiful shawl. The weave of the fabric was fine, and it was embroidered with two large peacocks.

"I embroidered one and Beatrice the other," Isobel explained. "I hope ye like it."

Cait hugged the item close to her chest and sniffed. "I cannot express how much I adore it."

At her happiness Isobel blinked, her eyes shiny with unshed tears. "Oh, Cait. I will miss ye."

"Do not make her cry," Lady Macdonald said nearing the bed.

Cait wasn't sure who she meant, but she nodded. "I will not make her cry."

"Not ye," the woman said. "I am speaking to Isobel. Do not make Cait cry, we cannot have a bride with red, swollen eyes tomorrow."

THE NEXT DAY, Stuart paced the length of the great room; he was growing tired of waiting for one thing or another. After first meal, he and Ewan had gone out to practice sword fighting to pass the time until the wedding, which was to take place in the late afternoon.

His squire, Anton, had run out and stopped him, stating his mother did not want him to be bruised or injured prior to the wedding. She'd then promptly had him bathe and dress, banishing him to the parlor to wait for whatever it was that he was to do next.

He spent the time thinking of that night and how he looked forward to having Cait beneath him again.

This time he wished to see all of her. When they'd made love the first time, she'd been reluctant to remove all her clothing. He was going to make sure that night both of them were free of every single piece of clothing. He would delight in her body, tasting every inch.

"Ye are aroused. It may not be a good idea to walk into the chapel like that," Caelan said, stating the obvious.

Stuart rubbed his hand down the front of his person, willing the member to soften. "How much longer and why am I to remain in here?"

"Yer mother does not wish for ye to see Cait until she walks into the chapel."

He looked out the window. "It should not be much longer."

"We are to walk to the chapel now." His brother motioned to the door. "Everyone is there."

"Caelan," Stuart began, "Do ye plan to marry?"

Caelan's gaze swept past him to the view outside "I do not know. I doubt it."

"Why?"

"Because I do not believe in love."

"Ye do not love me then?" Stuart asked smiling. "I am devastated."

Caelan looked up at the ceiling. "It is different with family. I care for ye and would die for ye. But to say that one feels so deeply for one woman. I find it impossible."

"Let us go," Stuart said and walked in front of his brother. He smiled hoping to be present when Caelan ate his words.

Once they arrived at the chapel, the room was crowded, every pew overflowing with family, friends, and villagers.

He'd asked Darach to stand with him, but his other brothers had decided among themselves that they'd also stand at the front. The only one not at the front of the chapel was Duncan, who could not abide small, cramped spaces. He stood at the back by the door, but Stuart knew that he was as happy for him as the other four were.

At the sight of his four brothers in their Ross tartans and crests, he had to blink back proud tears as he walked up and stood to wait.

There was a hush in the chapel, every head turning.

A resplendent Cait appeared at the doorway, it was as if all the air left his lungs. Stuart could not look away from the beauty that seemed to glide down the center of the church on her brother's arm. A proud Torac escorted his sister, his gaze straight ahead.

When they stopped at the front of the chapel, the warrior met his gaze. "Protect her always."

Throughout the entire service, Stuart could not pull his gaze from Cait. She was stunning. Her face was serene, but excitement shined from her eyes.

He could barely speak the vows, his voice shaking with

emotion. When Cait spoke hers, she smiled up at him as tears slipped down her cheeks.

When the cleric pronounced them husband and wife, his heart could barely contain the emotions. They walked out of the chapel, his hand on the small of her back protectively. This was the woman he would live out his days with and would never allow harm to come to.

A rush of pride came over him when he looked over and met Duncan's gaze. There was a sense of understanding, acknowledgement of how one becomes a better man with the right woman beside ye.

The guests followed them to the great hall that had been decorated with wildflowers and branches. It looked festive and he looked to Cait who took in the space.

"Is it not beautiful?" she asked in an awed tone. "This is much too special."

He pulled her against his side. "Ye deserve this and more."

The rest of the day was filled with revelry and celebration and it was a time that he vowed to keep in his memory forever.

When the musicians played a lively tune, Stuart partnered with his mother. They laughed the entire time while dancing, and when he stole a glance to Cait, she was smiling widely and clapping along.

A hush came over the crowd as Darach carried Isobel into the great room. Everyone cheered when she made a show of waving to them as they passed and settled at the high board.

Greer and her helpers outdid themselves with a wonderful feast. There was plenty of food for everyone to have their fill and wine was poured freely to those in attendance. By the time they finished eating and the music continued, Stuart noticed that Cait was tiring.

"Ye should see about the final celebration," his mother said as they walked back to the high board. "It is time for us to take Cait away."

Both of their mothers along with another pair of women ushered his blushing bride from the room.

"A toast," Darach announced.

As each of his brothers spoke and Stuart had to keep swallowing to keep from showing emotion. This was the end of a portion of his life.

Now it was time for him to forge ahead to what came next.

# CHAPTER TWENTY

"LAY STILL BENEATH him," her mother said. "It will be over soon enough." She blushed and patted Cait's shoulder. "Ye are attracted to him and that will help."

"Mother, ye act as if I am about to head to the gallows to be executed."

Her mother's eyes rounded and the other women in the room giggled.

"It should be very pleasant and enjoyable," Beatrice exclaimed. "If it is not let me know. I will ask Duncan to speak to him."

Ella laughed. "I believe we do not have to explain anything to her. Stuart has ensured she is well satisfied."

"Ella!" Lady Mariel looked to Cait's confused mother apologetically. "I am afraid my daughter has never been one to hold her tongue."

There were knocks at the door and loud cheerful voices.

"We must go." Beatrice and Ella pulled Lady Mariel and her mother out the door.

Moments later, Stuart was shoved in by a group of rowdy brothers, who laughed just a bit too loud.

Stuart's eyes narrowed and he turned to glare at his brothers. "Go away."

They exchanged a couple of crude barbs before finally

being pushed out and the door locked behind them.

"Sometimes we act like lads." Stuart smiled while shaking his head. "It is the first time we've had a proper wedding and I believe everyone is overly excited."

Cait sat in the bed hugging her legs up to her chest. "Everything has been so wonderful, but at times it felt as if the celebration had little to do with us. I believe everyone celebrated personal victories and that is quite extraordinary."

When he began to undress, she could not look away. She tried, but inevitably, her gaze would slide back. First, he sat and removed the boots, followed by stockings, and then his belt. He lowered his breeches and then sat down to pull them off.

Once that was done, he stood again. The pale linen tunic fell to just above his knees giving her glimpses of his muscled legs.

Stuart met her gaze. "I want to see ye remove that garment."

"I was told this is what men prefer," Cait replied, genuinely surprised. She had been led to believe, the man was always fully naked, and she would remain partially clothed.

"I prefer ye bare," he said as his fingers curled at the hem of the tunic. As the fabric inched upward, she followed the progress.

His muscular thighs were enticing. Between them his sex hung, nestled upon a plump sack. She watched with growing anticipation as his flat stomach and wide chest were exposed. When Stuart pulled the tunic off, he stood before her fully bare.

"Come," he held out a hand inviting her from the bed.

Cait obeyed, feeling a bit exposed despite wearing a night rail. It was made of fabric so thin, it was almost see-through.

"Ye are beautiful," Stuart proclaimed, his gaze raking over her. "I am a very fortunate man."

Taking a cue from his actions, Cait slowly untied the strips at the neck and pushed the garment down from her shoulders. It slid easily. Exposing her breasts. The dip of her waist. The flare of her hips.

Upon seeing her remove her nightgown, his sex hardened and lengthened. Breathlessly, Cait slowly pushed the night rail past her hips allowing it to slide down her legs to the floor.

There was something freeing when his gaze roamed over her body and she saw the arousal not only in his expression but the effect on his sex. It rose hardening before her eyes.

"I want ye so much right now," Stuart said, and she smiled in amazement that this beautiful man was her husband.

They came together with desperate need, touching, kissing, and caressing one another. Stuart took her body and in that moment the bond between them felt tangible. Cait cried out when she crested, her body tensing under his. He shuddered moments later, losing himself completely.

They lay there panting, the giddy feeling of two people who'd done something utterly enjoyable.

"I must ask ye something," Cait said, her voice sounding breathless. "Is this the only way?"

"What do ye mean?" Stuart lifted his head and gave her a curious look.

Cait shrugged. "Beatrice alluded to the fact that there were many ways to make love. I am curious."

When Stuart grinned, she knew it must be true.

He sat up and then looked at her for a moment as if gauging how to explain it. "Turn over onto yer stomach."

She did as he instructed, already feeling impatient to know what would happen next. He guided her to her knees and hands and moved to kneel behind her.

"What do ye think?" he asked in a husky voice.

Cait looked over her shoulder. "I am anxious to know what ye will do next."

Trailing his fingers from the nape of her neck, down her spine, Stuart continued until finding the entrance to her sex. "I will enter ye like this." He slipped a finger into her and she gasped.

She held her breath waiting to know how it would feel while he positioned himself and then slowly pushed in.

The intrusion was quite different, it was as if he was able to move deeper into her.

He then took her by the hips and began driving into her body over and over. Cait urged him to move faster, her mewls erupting of their own free will. She pushed back to meet his thrusts, enjoying the feel of his member so deep inside her. The sound of their skin slapping together was as erotic as Stuart's deep grunts.

Cait looked over her shoulder at the muscles of Stuart's shoulders and upper arms flexing with each movement. He watched where they came together, lips parted.

"Come for me, beauty," Stuart said slipping his hand from her hips to between her legs. It only took a few strokes against her most sensitive part before she dissolved, feeling as if she splintered into pieces.

"Oh!" Cait cried out her head falling forward onto the

bedding. Stuart was unrestrained, his fingers digging into her hips to hold her in place as he plunged in again and again. Cait was lost in the moment, her pliant body controlled by Stuart's movements.

It was as if he'd lost control. He then turned her so that he could stand beside the bed and continued driving into her.

His breathing was harsh as he continued to take her harder, faster. Cait cried out again, she could not hold onto reality and finally lost control. As everything became dark, stars swirled around her. In the darkness, she heard Stuart's growl and then felt heated liquid spill into her core.

She allowed the promise of darkness to pull her under as Stuart cradled her against him whispering soft words that were like tender caresses.

THE NEXT MORNING, Cait woke first. Her body felt like liquid and a bit tender in parts. Her legs were wobbly like jelly when she rose to relieve herself and her inner thighs showed light bruising.

The aftereffects of their lovemaking however made her smile. It was a delicious soreness that brought instant memories of what had happened between them.

She studied the slumbering man in the bed. He slept on his stomach, facing her. The dark waves of hair a tousled mess. The strands spread over the side of his face and shoulders. He was a sensual picture with the blankets pulled down showing her just a peek at his bottom. Though the wide expanse of his back was just as enticing. And the fact he was so evenly tanned, made her wonder how much time he spent outdoors devoid of clothing.

She slipped into the bed and pressed a kiss to his jaw.

Stuart's eyes opened and he smiled at her. "Is it morning already?"

"It is," Cait replied snuggling against him. "But I plan to sleep a bit more."

LATER THAT MORNING when Stuart's hands slid over her, Cait opened her eyes to find him positioned between her legs. "We cannot possibly..." She stopped talking and took a sharp breath noting how aroused he was.

He made love to her gently. His movements so slow and precise he sent her into a place so glorious, she would never have believed it existed.

When they finished, they lay in each other's arms until there was a soft knock on the door.

Stuart got up from the bed and wrapped his tartan around himself.

"I brought some ale and food for ye to break yer fast," Cora announced. She walked in and quickly placed a tray on the table.

Thankfully she did not look toward the bed, but instead, turn and walked back out.

"It smells wonderful," Cait said slipping from the bed. She tugged on a robe and went to sit next to the fireplace as Stuart added wood to it. It was strange to be alone with him for so long and at the same time she wondered how long it would be like this, so new and exciting.

He lowered to a chair and lifted a cup to drink. "What are ye thinking? Ye are so quiet."

"It feels odd, to be alone with ye. I am so very happy right now." She met his gaze and tingles traveled through her.

Stuart smiled. "I agree, it is different. Spending time alone together will ease us into our marriage." He looked around. "Once we eat, what do ye wish to do?"

Cait giggled and looked to the bed. "We could sleep a bit."

They slept until later in the day and once they woke, Stuart dressed and stood at the window. Cait brushed her hair while watching him in the mirror. "When do ye wish to return to... Do yer lands have a name?"

"Aye, *Eilean Daes*," he responded with a wide smile. "Lovely Isle."

"I like it. Yer mother says there is a huge loch nearby."

"Loch Bee and a smaller one as well."

"I wonder why Keep Ross was not built there?" Cait mused.

Stuart shrugged. "At one time, my great-grandfather and his brother split the isle. One living here and the other up there in the larger house."

"Did ye ever live there while growing up?"

Her new husband shook his head. "No. My grandfather moved there eventually, giving lairdship over to my father. We visited on occasion."

"Interesting," Cait said.

Stuart stretched. "I never found out why my grandfather gave up lairdship. At times I wonder if my father had something to do with it."

Cait had heard that the late laird was not well-liked and noted that the family rarely spoke about him. This was the first time Stuart mentioned him and she decided not to ask any more questions about him. "What should we do until last meal?" she asked.

Her husband turned from the window meeting her gaze. "I do not know."

"What if we sneak out and go for a walk. It looks rather sunny outside."

Stuart looked to the door, his lips curving. "We will be caught."

"I find it hard to believe that as young lads ye and yer brothers did not have ways to escape without anyone seeing ye."

His face brightened when a thought came.

"Come, I know a way to avoid the others." He took her hand and they walked out of the room. Once in the corridor, Stuart guided her down to a dark corner. Then he pushed at what looked like a wall and it slid open.

"There may be some bad smells," he warned, before pulling her into the darkness behind him. They crept down steps and he reached out for a torch. Moments later the flame lit their way.

"How did ye light it?" Cait wasn't sure why she whispered.

"Flint," he replied holding up a small stone. "It is kept here in case there's need for a fast escape."

Then moments later, the distinctive salty smell let her know they reached the sea. When Stuart opened a second door, they were in a small cave. He placed the torch into a holder as they no longer needed it and guided her past a pair of boats and out to the open field beside the house.

"I knew it," Cait said with a smile. "I came here to the side of the house one day and saw the boats. I wondered if there was a hidden entrance into the house."

"Who goes there!" a stern voice called out and moments later a pair of guards with swords drawn appeared. The men relaxed upon seeing it was Stuart.

One of them gave them a knowing look. "Escaping the confines of the marriage chamber so soon?"

"I required fresh air," Cait replied.

"And the window is quite small," Stuart said with a grin.

*A fortnight later.*

THE PACKING WAS complete. Already a pair of wagons had left for *Eilean Daes.*

In the sitting room, Cait sorted through several baskets. "I cannot believe all these things are wedding gifts," she repeated. "For us."

Lady Mariel sniffed. "I cannot believe ye are leaving so soon. I will miss ye dear lass."

As excited as she was to leave, Cait dreaded having to say farewell to the people at Keep Ross she'd grown so close to.

But after hugging Lady Mariel, Beatrice, and Isobel, she then went down the stairs to find Annis, Greer, and Finella. Every single one of them made her cry as they wished her happiness and a great new life.

She was almost grateful that Stuart sought her out and announced it was time to head out if they were to arrive by sundown.

Already her brother, Brice, had left with one of the wagons and a pair of horses he planned to breed. Her mother and Cora were already inside the carriage when Stuart helped Cait inside.

Eyes bright with excitement, her mother patted her leg. "Can ye believe it lass? We are to move once again. To start anew and this time to live a privileged life."

Cait reached to touch her mother, noting her hand shook. "I am still waiting to wake from this wonderful dream."

Stuart was to ride ahead of the party with three warriors, there were an additional four guardsmen behind the carriage and one on either side.

As they headed away, Cait stuck her head out the window to peer at Keep Ross. The beautiful structure became smaller and smaller as they rode away, and she sighed silently thanking it for the time there.

"Did ye see Torac?" Cait asked her mother. "I sent someone with a message, but he never came."

"He is right there." Her mother pointed to the opposite side of where she'd been looking. Cait slid to the other side and peered up to see that her half brother rode atop his huge warhorse beside the carriage.

Torac glanced at her and nodded.

"Is he to live at *Eilean Daes* as well?" Cait looked to Cora, who pretended to not be listening.

Her mother shook her head. "I asked him, but he plans to return in a few days. The reason he came was to ensure our safety. I am sure Brice asked him to come along. He has developed a rather strong attachment to his older brother."

"Oh, Cora, how do ye feel? I know ye were looking forward to not seeing him daily."

Her friend let out a long breath. "I suppose it will be only temporary. I will have to do my best to keep my distance from him."

It was quite late by the time they arrived at *Eilean Daes*. Cait and Cora looked out to the passing shoreline of a large loch on one side and the sea was visible in the distance on the other side.

The carriage slowed down as they traversed the uneven road to a path between tall trees. Upon arriving at a large clearing, a house on a hill surrounded by sheep, large planting fields, and corrals with horses came into view. There were several other structures that included stables, guard quarters, and a smaller house.

When they neared the front of the house, the driver pulled the horses to a stop.

"I can barely keep from throwing myself out the door and begin exploring," Cait exclaimed clasping her hands together.

They remained seated in the carriage, until the servants finished lining up just outside the front door.

Torac opened the door and helped them from the carriage. Just as Cait stepped onto the ground Stuart joined them. He took her elbow and Torac took her mothers and together they went to the line of servants and were introduced.

Two women, who were the housekeeper and the cook, Maisie and Grace, beamed at her. "Finally, ye arrive Mistress," Grace exclaimed with a bright smile.

"We have been anxious to meet ye," Maisie said by way of greeting.

Other than the two women, there was only one other woman, Bree, who lived on the property. Bree was married to Stuart's cousin, Dougal. Apparently back at Keep Rosss, they'd been living in the village, which was why Cait had never met her.

Bree was soft-spoken and seemed sweet. "I am glad that ye are here," she told Cait.

There were several guards and a stable worker, as well as Brice, Anton, and Lyall that rounded out those who would live there.

Once inside, Cait was shocked at how beautiful the house was. It was spacious, with high ceilings and large hearths in every room. The great room was divided by a half wall with an arched doorway. On one side a gathering room, on the other a large dining room.

She allowed Stuart to take her to their bedchamber as Bree went with her mother and Cora to show them theirs.

The room was large with shuttered windows that looked out to what Stuart had described as a future flower garden. Currently, the soil was tilled but nothing was planted. In the bedchamber there was a large four-poster bed, a small fireplace, and in one corner there was a screen for privacy. Also, a large wardrobe dominated one wall, and her trunk joined his at the foot of the bed.

Two chairs with a table between them faced the fireplace and there was a small table on each side of the bed.

"The room is beautiful," Cait said, and meant she it. "The house is well built and every aspect of it quite pleasing."

She opened her mouth to tell him that she wished to have been part of it, to have helped rebuild the home back to its former beauty, but he hugged her close. "I did this for ye."

Cait held her tongue as he took her hand to show her more of the house.

After she had a chance to wash up and change, they went to the dining room as Maisie and Grace were quite anxious to serve them their first meal.

They sat at a table with her mother, Torac, and Lyall. Cora chose to stay in the kitchen and Cait understood her not wishing to eat in the same room as Torac.

Moments after they sat and began nibbling from a platter of cheese and fruit, Bree and Dougal joined them.

The cooks bustled out to serve each a large bowl of rich stew with warm baked bread and freshly churned butter. The meal was wonderful and Cait informed the women that she enjoyed every bite.

"How fares Artair?" Stuart asked his cousin.

Dougal shook his head. "He is most anxious for ye to appoint someone else to the post. Says he cannot abide village life."

"Tomorrow Cait and I go to the village. I will give her the choice of continuing to live here or there. The house there is most spacious."

Cait gave him a curious look. "I cannot imagine living in a village. I can already tell ye that I will prefer to remain here. However, if there are duties to be performed, then I will go wherever ye decide is best."

When he gave her a warm look, her insides melted.

"What about ye Bree?" Stuart asked. "How do ye feel about living in the village?"

Dougal gave Stuart an incredulous look. "Do ye mean for me to take over as constable?"

"Only if Bree wishes to live in the ostentatious house in the village."

Bree giggled. “I must admit to finding the house quite out of place. Almost like a castle amongst shacks. It looks quite strange.”

“Can anything be changed about it?” Cait asked. “I would not wish to live in a place that would make those around me feel less than.”

“Quite so,” Bree agreed, then her eyes widened as she addressed her husband. “Would we live there if ye is to become constable?”

Everyone paused when Dougal shrugged. “I am not sure. What say ye, Stuart?”

“I will leave it up to ye. But it is a grand house.”

The interest was obvious when Dougal looked to his wife. “Would ye live there?”

Bree waved his worry away. “I would. However, we must find a way to make it more welcoming. Perhaps house orphans or something.”

“Off to find orphans then,” Dougal announced, and everyone chuckled.

# CHAPTER TWENTY-ONE

THE PARTY OF five rode to the village the following day. While the men rode horses, Cait, Bree, and Cora rode in a carriage. Although Cait had recently learned to ride, Bree was not at ease doing so.

"Oh goodness, how quaint," Cait said as the village came into view. "This isn't at all what I expected. Although the homes and shops are clustered together—like most villages—here all of them face the sea."

There was one road along the shoreline, lined with small buildings, and a second one on higher ground with more cottages.

"I find it pretty," Bree said with a smile. "I suppose that's good as it is to become my home." Peering out the window, she pointed. "There it is."

A large stone house with a wall around it and ornate gates stood atop a small hill overlooking the village. There were a few sheep grazing inside the wall, and a pair of horses in the back area. Cait supposed one was Artair's.

"It is protected," Cait said, not sure she could find anything positive to say about the way it did not seem to fit with its surroundings.

The brick structure looked strong, so at least there was that. She looked to Bree who also studied the house. "Ye will not have to worry when a storm comes. Ye can offer harbor to the villagers."

Bree frowned. "Honestly, I am not sure how I feel about living there. The people may not accept me."

"I am sure once they get to know ye, they will soften swiftly. Ye should host a gathering for women. Good food melts many a reserve."

Bree brightened. "That is a fabulous idea."

"I will come and help ye," Cora added.

Once arriving at the village, the women went to the square. Cait introduced herself and Bree followed suit. They found a pair of women who sold baskets and other trinkets. The women were quite talkative. Cait was sure not long after she and Bree walked away, they would inform the entire village of their conversation.

"Miss Bree Ross and her husband Mister Dougal Ross will be moving into the large house on the hill," Cait told the women, who leaned forward in anticipation of being the first to hear the news.

"If ye are aware of someone wishing to work there, inform me," Bree added. "I will be hiring a pair of hands to assist with cooking and cleaning. My husband will also be seeking help with the surrounding lands. We will offer fair pay."

The women grinned with glee and shoved their purchases into their arms in an obvious attempt to get rid of them so they could spread the news.

By the time they reached the last shop, several women had already approached Bree asking questions. And across the square where Stuart and Dougal spoke to Artair, men had gathered as well.

Cait stopped listening to the women gathered, to study Stuart. He stood listening to the men, his shoulders back. The men gathered often bowed their heads when addressing him as he had an air of authority. The sea air blew his hair away from his handsome face and she noted how at ease he seemed.

It was as if he was meant to be here, with people that were eager for fair leadership.

"My husband will enjoy duties of constable. He has always admired Stuart's even nature and his ability to give good counsel," Bree told her.

"There is so much about him I have yet to learn," Cait replied.

"It can be quite a journey," Bree said looking across toward Dougal.

When they made it to the house, the anticipation of what would be inside was tangible.

The house was large and overly decorated. Both Bree and Cora yelped several times when stepping on a rug that still had the animal's head attached.

"Those must be removed at once," Bree said with a shudder. "The bear is staring right at me."

Cait laughed when Bree hurried around the dead animal.

Once they completed the tour, it was decided that Dougal and Bree would move into it within the week.

Artair would move into the small house at *Eilean Daes* that they currently lived in.

On the ride back to their home, Bree talked excitedly about her upcoming move, making mental lists of what she needed to change in the house. Cait felt a bit tired, so she allowed her eyes to close while Cora spoke with Bree.

When they arrived back at the house, Cait felt refreshed. She went in search of her mother to inform her that the next day, they would help Bree pack.

Her mother was in her bedchamber, sitting in a chair with her arms crossed. She glared up at her when she walked in.

Alarmed, Cait hurried closer. "Is something wrong? Are ye ill?"

"No," her mother said. "I feel perfectly fine, do not worry over me." She motioned to a rather oversized bouquet of wildflowers, artfully set in a pitcher with springs of berries sticking out from several sides.

"Is there something crawling on the flowers?"

"No. Grace put it together, I am sure she ensured nothing harmful is in them."

"Why does a beautiful bouquet of flowers annoy ye Mother?" Cait gave her a worried look. "Should I worry about yer mind?"

"For goodness' sake." Her mother huffed indignantly. "That man, Lyall, he collected them and handed them to me in front of Maisie and Grace. I was mortified at his frivolous display."

When Cait giggled, her mother glared. "It is not in the least bit funny Cait. He should be banned from entering the house."

"Mother, he is a Ross and therefore cannot be banned. If ye wish, I will speak to him and let him know ye do not wish his attentions."

Her mother considered it for a moment. "That is a good idea."

CAIT ENJOYED LAST meal though admittedly, she was anxious

to spend time alone with Stuart. She ordered a bath so that once the meal was over, she could wash up before bed.

"I will have one as well," Stuart told her. "I smell of horse and fish. Did ye see the fishermen ask me to come and see their catch? They had quite a few fish."

"I am well aware of it, husband, as ye insisted we bring those they gave ye in the carriage," Cate grumbled.

"Did ye enjoy traveling to the village today?" Stuart asked as they climbed into the bed after their baths.

"I did, and look forward to going often," Cait replied with a smile. She moved closer to Stuart. "There was something about ye that was different when ye were there."

"Different? How?"

"Ye looked as if it was the place ye belong. That yer destiny is to be here and along with yer cousins attend to the needs of these poor people who have been neglected and mistreated for far too long."

"They were eager to speak to us," Stuart said. "I found that despite what happened with the constable, they are willing to trust me."

Cait kissed him. "I am very proud of ye."

"I realize it was a long day, but I am hoping that ye are not too tired." Stuart nuzzled her neck. "Seeing ye bathe brought me to arousal and I nearly pulled ye from the water to have ye."

Instead of a reply, Cait shifted and pressed her body against his. "I am not tired at all."

TWO DAYS LATER, loud wind and rain pelted the house with force. The men rushed out to ensure the horses and smaller livestock were sheltered in the stables. Although sheep were smart enough to huddle under a shelter of some sort, men went in search of any who might've become lost.

A rider arrived, shivering, and soaked through. He was rushed into the kitchen so that he could warm up by the large hearth and given hot herbs to drink to dispel the chill.

"The storm has hit the village. Houses are washed away along with some of the people. Help is needed."

"All of the men are gone to collect the sheep," Bree explained.

"I believe Torac stayed behind," Cait hurried through the house, hoping to find her brother.

When she went to the small bedchamber next to her mother's she knocked and Torac opened the door. He'd been out in the rain and had just changed into dry clothes. Cait hated to give him news, which would take him back out into the storm.

"The village is being washed away. They require rescue," she said, already tears streaming down her face. "Those poor, poor people."

Torac turned away and grabbed a cloak. "We will save those who have survived. Do not worry."

Thankfully the others returned not much later with the sheep they'd found. The animals protested at being ushered into shelter but seemed to settle quickly upon noticing the feed.

Soaked to the skin, Stuart waved at her. "Do not come out," he shouted when she went to grab her cloak.

"I love ye," Cait said wondering if he heard her through the hard rain.

The group of men mounted to head to the village, leaving the women behind to care for the animals and the house.

THE WIND AND rain were relentless. Stuart thought he'd go blind from trying to see the way. It took much longer than it should have for him and the others to arrive at the village. At least they thought it was the village, it was hard to tell because huge waves slammed far past the shoreline.

They stopped atop the hill, taking shelter under a stall next to one of the houses that had been spared.

Some cottages that were closer to the edge of the hill had slid down the saturated land taking everything those who lived in them owned. And in some cases, the owners themselves.

After a few moments of rest, they rode on. As they made their way down the coastline, they gathered people seeking refuge and took them to the main house. There Artair was already housing dozens of women and children, and any men too old or too ill to be out searching for their neighbors. The location of the home was far enough from the village below to keep it from any real damage. The tall walls and sturdy house offered protection to those that had managed to get there.

Carrying two young lads and a dog they refused to leave behind on his horse, Stuart arrived at the house.

Artair who was drenched and muddy hurried the children inside. "Where are yer parents?" he yelled over the loud wind. The boys shook their heads, and the one clinging to the shivering pup began to cry.

The older one looked toward the door. "Father was out there fishing. Mum went to see about him, and we saw a wave take her."

A woman came and took the lads, ushering them to the hearth. "We will find ye a blanket to keep warm," she said soothingly.

Searching for the lost and attempting to keep from being washed away themselves, took all their strength as they continued to trudge out to help save villagers.

By the time darkness fell, Stuart was too exhausted to keep going. And it was becoming much too dangerous to continue the search. Even though the sea had calmed some, the rain and wind continued unabated.

He'd just sat down to rest and drink some hot tea when someone began pounding on the front door.

Stuart rose and partially opened the door, trying to keep the cold wind and rain from blowing inside. On the other side of the door stood a man frantically motioning for Stuart to come outside.

"My wife," the man yelled to be heard over the storm. "I need help. She is trapped and will drown if we don't save her."

Stuart looked around at all the exhausted men and checking his own reserve he turned back to the man and tried to explain. "We are all too exhausted, I do not know what help we can be to ye." He paused and looked around the room again. "We simply haven't the strength. And I cannot risk another life by sending them back out. It's just too dangerous.

The man's face fell, and there was desperation in his gaze when he looked at Stuart. "Help me, sir. I beg of ye. I cannot let her die. She is my world."

When Stuart hesitated, the man turned and walked back into the storm.

Stuart closed his eyes. If it were Cait, he would not rest until he saved her.

"Wait," he called out to the man.

Stuart went inside, grabbed a rope and his still soaked tartan, and went back out.

# CHAPTER TWENTY-TWO

IT WAS LATE the next day before any news about the village reached Cait. A pair of guards arrived with a wagonload of people to shelter there.

The two families were given dry clothing and fed. They were to stay at Dougal and Bree's house until the weather calmed, then husbands would return to the village to rebuild their homes.

Through tears, the women told Cait about how many homes had been washed away and of several people who were still missing.

The villagers had come together, with those who still had homes standing welcoming those misfortunate ones who didn't. Children who could not find their parents were at the house on the hill along with any families in need of a healer.

Bree immediately decided she would take blankets and dry clothing for the people.

"I will go as well," Cait declared. "We cannot sit idly by and do nothing."

A look of alarm crossed the guard's face, who'd brought the people. "I do not think ye should go. There is scarcely any room for those there at the house."

"We will find a spot with our husbands," Cait told the man who shook his head firmly.

"Ye should remain here. We may bring more."

"Nonsense," Bree said with a firm shake of her head. "That is to be my home, I have to help."

The man looked to Cait. "Then perhaps just Lady Ross should stay here."

Cait stilled and studied the man for a long beat. "Did my husband insist ye do not bring me there?"

"I have not spoken to him, Lady Ross. I was told by Mister Artair to ensure ye did not come."

"Did he tell ye this without my husband knowing?"

The guard swallowed and remained silent.

"Where is my husband?" Cait asked, her heart thundering as a sense of dread began to suffocate her. "Where is Stuart?" she whispered.

"I do not know," the guard admitted. "He went to help someone rescue their wife and did not return."

It was as if the earth yanked her down because suddenly Cait's knees gave way and she sunk to the floor. Instantly, Cora and Bree were at her side.

"Are they searching for him?" Bree asked.

The guard looked even more exhausted than when he arrived. "All I know is that he was not at the house. I was busy helping people and overheard someone say they were searching for him. That he'd not been seen since last night."

"We will leave at once," Cait said, gaining strength. "Immediately."

The women rushed around the house, throwing blankets into the carriage.

It wasn't long before they were racing as fast as was safe on the muddy roads toward the village.

Cait did not cry. She refused to believe that so soon after their marriage, her husband had been washed out to sea. His life lost at the place he seemed to have finally found himself.

Life could not possibly be so cruel.

Seeming to sense that she could not speak, Cora and Bree let her be and went over what supplies they'd brought, doing their best to arrange things in the cramped space.

It was as the guard had described, utter devastation. The village was unrecognizable from just a few days ago when they'd arrived.

There were a few people milling about, digging in the sand and debris probably searching for lost belongings.

A lone boy sat on a hill overlooking the sea with his head bowed. "Ye should go see about him," Cait told Bree, who knocked on the roof of the carriage indicating the driver should stop. The man came to the door but did not let them out.

That is Tom, his brother is at the house. He looks for his parents, they were both lost in the storm.

"The poor wee thing," Bree said with a hitch in her voice. "Please continue until we see those out searching for Stuart."

A short time later, the carriage came to a stop and an angry Torac appeared. He was drenched and muddy.

"Why are ye here?" he glared at her and Cora. "There is enough to worry about without ye all here."

"Where is Stuart?" Cait said ignoring his outburst. "Where is my husband?"

Torac didn't reply, instead he called up to the driver to take them to the house.

"No," Cait screamed. "Tell me right now Torac. Where is

Stuart?" Panic set in and she could barely breathe. "The truth."

Torac met her gaze. "We are searching the shoreline. He went to help a man whose wife was trapped. We do not know where she was, or in what direction they went. All we know is that the man lived in that direction." Torac pointed forward. "I am riding in the opposite direction in case he was dragged out by the tide."

"Do ye think he is dead?"

Her brother took a deep breath. "It would be a miracle if he is not."

For some reason instead of making her upset, his honesty helped her settle. "I believe in miracles," she said meeting his gaze. "Have any of the items taken by the storm washed back up on the shore?"

"Aye," Torac said once again pointing in the direction they headed. "Mostly up there."

Cait called up to the driver. "Go."

When they arrived where the others were searching for Stuart, her heart sank. The shoreline was rocky and hard to traverse. Everyone was on foot as horses would get their hooves caught in the rocks.

Upon seeing them, Artair and Dougal hurried over. Neither chastised them, instead asked that they stay together and help search.

It was a long time later that despair began to inch its way inside. Tears poured down her face when a young man's mangled body was recovered. He'd washed ashore while they searched. They took him and placed him next to the bodies of two others.

Someone yelled stating they'd found someone alive. Her

hopes soared only to be dashed, when two guards appeared with a woman who had survived but was badly bruised. She was ushered into the carriage.

"Ye should return to the house with her. Ye need to eat," Artair told Cait. "I will continue searching through the night."

"I cannot leave," Cait said, looking up at the sky and glad to see that clouds were not gathering. "I have to stay and look."

A bonfire was lit and soon the fire burned brightly.

Despite the fact she was quickly losing energy, she forced herself to walk away from the fire's warmth and back in the direction of where the woman had been found.

Dougal caught up with her, his face haggard from lack of sleep. "If I know my cousin, he dragged himself under some brush and is covered with branches to keep warm. Which increases his chances of surviving but makes it harder to find him if he is unconscious."

The words made her feel better as they continued searching on the beach where the waves now lapped peacefully against the rocks.

"There's something," Dougal said and scrambled to pull a sodden tartan from the water. It was Stuart's.

Cait's eyes widened as she scanned the shoreline expecting to see Stuart's lifeless body. In desperation, she raced down to the water looking side to side, for any sign of him.

"Stuart!" she screamed. Her cries were muffled by the sound of the sea. "Stuart!" Stumbling across the rocks, she walked back into the woods praying to find something that indicated he survived.

"Look!" Dougal exclaimed rushing toward some bushes. In his hurry, he tripped and as he scrambled to stand, Cait caught up with him. She didn't see anything.

"What is it?" She shook with fear. Torn between wanting to know the truth and at the same time fearing it.

"There," Dougal said rushing forward to where it looked as if a tree had fallen. He pulled an oversized branch and there on the ground curled into a ball was a man's body.

"Who is it?" Cait asked suddenly barely able to put one foot in front of the other. Dougal was bent over the person touching him and then he removed his thick coat and placed it over the man.

When he looked to Cait, he was crying. "It is him. He is barely alive."

Cait threw herself over Stuart willing the little bit of body heat she had to seep into him. "Go get help," she screamed.

Dougal rushed off yelling for help. She removed her cloak and then her underskirts and did her best to wrap Stuart with them. His lips were blue and his breathing shallow, but he was alive and that was all that mattered.

DAYS PASSED AND Stuart remained unconscious. They kept him at the large house in the village at first. However, after a pair of days, she and her mother decided to take him home. If he were to die, Cait preferred that he spend his last days in their new home.

He'd regained his coloring and his breathing normalized, but he did not waken. Every day Cait would spend a long time painstakingly feeding him clear broths and herbal teas so that he had some nutrition. Even though she was as careful as she could be, at times he would choke on what she gave him. It was the only time he seemed to have a bit of life in him. Coughing and sputtering. It was what kept her going. The belief that he was still in there and he would beat this.

Every day she sat beside him, speaking to him. Every night she would cuddle with him, kissing his face and reassuring him that she loved him.

IT WASN'T UNTIL the day that the rest of the family arrived that reality sunk in. Stuart, in all probability, would die. Cait went into mourning. She hid from everyone. Stayed with her mother and allowed the brothers and Lady Mariel to take turns watching over Stuart.

Once they had all sought their beds for the night, only then would she go to the bedchamber and sleep with him.

One morning, Cait walked in from breaking her fast to find Lady Mariel attempting to feed Stuart. The liquid was spilling from his mouth down his chin.

"He does not like that," Cait snapped, taking the spoon and bowl from the startled woman. "Ye must feed him slower."

Cait put the items aside and wiped Stuart's chin with great care.

"Have ye told him that he can go?" Lady Mariel asked, her eyes tearing up. "He may be waiting to hear those words from ye."

"He cannot go," Cait replied curtly. "He will recover. It will take time, but that is why I feed him and have the guards come in daily and sit him up in the chair. The healer told me it is important that he be able to sit and use his legs."

Lady Mariel studied her son's face and smiled at him. "I wish ye would open yer eyes." She told him. And then looked to Cait. "He has the most beautiful eyes of all my sons. They all have bright green with bits of blue and gold, but Stuart has the most gold of all of them."

"Aye, he does," Cait replied glad Lady Mariel did not speak again of allowing Stuart to die.

When Cait began to feed him, the woman walked out to give her time alone with him.

Moments later, she placed the bowl and spoon aside and lifted his right arm and flexed it several times. His limbs were heavy, and she loved that about him.

Cait bent and placed a kiss on his mouth. "Why do ye not waken my love?" She lowered his right arm and began working with the left. "It has been four weeks. Ye have had yer rest. I need ye to wake."

His eyes fluttered. Sometimes when she spoke to him, they did that, but they never opened.

"I was hoping to tell ye once ye were awake and looking at me, but I cannot keep it to myself any longer," Cait said releasing his arm.

Cupping his face with her hands, she studied his face. "Ye are going to be a father, Stuart. I am with child."

Her breath caught when he didn't respond. "Waken my love, I cannot do it by myself. I do not want to raise our bairn alone. Please do not leave me."

She wiped tears away, but more followed so quickly in their wake she gave up. "Now that I found ye, I do not want to be without ye. I cannot let ye go. I refuse to do it."

Unable to withstand the silence and lack of reaction, she

raced from the room and out the front door into the nearby trees to cry in private. Rain began to fall but Cait didn't care. She could not return to the house. To the reality that her husband was dying. And to the family who walked about draped in grief waiting for the inevitable.

It was a long while later that she trudged back to the house. Straightening, Cait did her best to gain strength to face what was her life now.

Darach Ross stood in the doorway looking in her direction. His blond mane was being tossed in the wind making him look like his moniker. A lion.

That he watched her approach could only mean there was news and she braced herself.

"Something happened?" she asked just a few paces from the doorway, unwilling to take another step.

"He was thrashing about violently," Darach replied and wiped a tear away. "We had to tie him down."

Cait began to cry. "I must go see about him."

"Do ye really believe he will recover?" the proud laird asked, searching her face. "Ye cling to a hope that I wish I had."

"Hope is all I have." She fell against him, and he hugged her. The feel of the large man's body was so much like Stuart's that she wanted to cling to him and pretend it was Stuart if only for a little while.

Letting out a sigh, she pushed away and went into the house and straight to her and Stuart's bedchamber.

# CHAPTER TWENTY-THREE

THE SURROUNDINGS DID not resemble anything he recalled. His body felt heavy and cumbersome, and when he tried to roll to his side it was impossible.

He had to relieve himself badly, but when he tried to sit, it was as if he was held down.

Stuart tried to lift his right arm. He could not, it was so heavy that a grunt escaped.

Cait slept soundly next to him, with her back to him. He hated to wake her. However, it was better to wake and ask for help than to urinate on her.

"Caith," his tongue did not cooperate. It was as if he'd drunk too much the night before. "Caith," he repeated louder "Wake."

His wife jerked and sat up with a start, her eyes wide. "Stuart?"

"I n-neeth to... relieve myself. I cannot... move," he said getting a bit impatient at his uncooperative tongue. "Am I tieth up?"

"Ye are," Cait said slowly. "Ye were thrashing about and yer brothers were afraid ye would hurt yerself." She began to cry.

"Ye are awake," she whispered.

"Why... are ye... crying?" What was happening? It was as

if time had passed without him and he had no idea why.

"I will fetch Darach or Ewan."

She raced from the room calling out his brothers' names. When had his brothers arrived?

Moments later the room became crowded, the bed surrounded by grinning loons.

"If ye… do not helth me up. I am going to lay… in my own piss," he stuttered, with annoyance.

"Why all the crying?" he asked as Darach untied him.

Duncan appointed himself assistant to help him relieve himself. He pulled Stuart from the bed and half-carried him to the corner behind the screen. When his brother reached between his legs, Stuart swatted his hand away clumsily. "I can do ith myself."

"No, ye cannot," Duncan said and when Stuart tried to take a step forward, his legs would not hold him up. Luckily his larger brother easily kept him from falling and held him up while helping Stuart to manage his business.

When he was returned to the bed, Stuart frowned at those surrounding him. "What happened to me?"

"We thought ye were going to die." His mother wrapped her arms around his shoulders and kissed his head. She began to sob and one of his other brothers pulled her away.

"I did not expect ye would," Gideon said with a look of superiority. "I was just telling Ewan and Duncan that earlier."

"Ye said ye wanted these lands," Duncan said shoving the youngest aside so he could stare at Stuart. "What do ye remember?"

Stuart frowned looking around the room for Cait but did not see her. "I remember going to the village to help after the storm."

Before he could ask, Caelan peered around Duncan's shoulder. "They are making great headway in rebuilding. This time the houses are being built on higher ground. All that remains on the lower road are some of the shacks used by the fishermen."

As Caelan spoke Stuart could not bring himself to ask the obvious.

Thankfully his brothers always seemed to read one another's minds.

"Ye have been unconscious for a long time. It has been almost a month since Dougal and Cait found ye."

"I do not remember anything."

"Perhaps ye will soon enough," Cait said appearing and coming to his side, her face blotchy from crying.

"Ye need rest and food," his mother added her reddened eyes boring into him.

Maisie entered with a tray of broth and some warm tea. Though his insides felt so hollow he'd have much rather had a big bowl of hearty stew followed by a tankard of dark ale, his mother gave him no choice in the matter. And she banned everyone from his room saying he needed to rest, but he knew it was so his brothers couldn't slip him any forbidden food.

Despite him arguing against it, his wife insisted on feeding him. And even though he felt near to starving, his stomach only allowed him to take in a bit before it began to protest. To distract him as she fed him, Cait told him all that had happened, not sparing any detail. Drained by all that he learned and by all that had occurred, he fell asleep holding her hand, asking that she not leave his side.

IT'D BEEN SEVERAL weeks since Stuart woke. His mother and brothers had remained another sennight to reassure themselves that he would fully recover. With each passing day he regained his strength, but he never regained his memory of what had occurred. She sometimes wondered if it was a way of his mind protecting itself against what he had witnessed that night.

They'd learned that the man who he'd gone to help, as well as his wife, had perished the night of the storm. Miraculously, only five people in total had died. The couple Stuart had tried to help. The young boy, Tom's parents. And the young man that washed up on the beach while Cait and Dougal searched for Stuart.

Pushing the bad memories aside, Cait reluctantly peered out the window of the carriage and was pleasantly surprised at the view that met her on the way to the village.

Some new homes had been finished. Others were still in process. But the men made sure each new roof was rainproof.

She looked to Stuart who stared intently in the direction of the sea. "Look," she said, pointing just off the coast where a pair of small boats bobbed. "Life is going back to normal. It is the way of things in a seaside village. These are resilient people."

HE TURNED AND met her gaze. "Ye are like them. Strong and brave. I would not be alive if it was not for yer determination. Mother told me she'd asked that ye allow me to die and ye would not accept it."

"She feels horrible," Cait replied. "It was painful either way. To see ye suffering was almost more horrible than the idea of ye dying."

His hand covered hers and he leaned forward to kiss her. "Ye seem different."

Cait cocked her head to the side. "Do I?" She gave him a warm smile, knowing he'd wonder what she left unsaid.

Since he'd woken, she'd not found the opportunity to tell him about their child. They'd yet to make love and she couldn't help but wonder if Stuart found he could not.

That night, she vowed to reassure him that all would be well. Even if they could no longer make love, not in the traditional way, they were blessed with a child and her love for him would never diminish.

Upon their arrival at the house on the hill, Bree welcomed them with a warm smile as Tom, his younger brother, Ian, and the dog raced out of the house to find adventure. She threaded her arm through Cait's, and they headed to the sitting room. While Stuart went in search of Artair—who'd traveled ahead—and Dougal. The men were to meet regularly to go over village concerns.

"How are ye doing?" Bree asked. "Have ye felt the babe move yet? It should be like the fluttering of butterfly wings."

Bree had a son, who was almost twenty. The young man had remained behind at Keep Ross working.

"I think so," Cait said automatically placing her hand over her stomach. "I have decided to tell Stuart tonight."

Bree smiled. "Take yer time. Ye have both been through a great ordeal." Her friend looked out through the window. "I worry about the lads. They have their sad moments and Tom is overly protective of Ian."

"They are fortunate to have ye and Dougal as parents now," Cait reassured her. "I am sure they will never forget their first parents, but ye will be their new mother. It was nice to see the smiles on their faces just now."

THEY SPENT THE rest of the day there. When Cait and Bree walked through the village, it was reassuring to see that the people had settled back into their daily lives.

ON THE RIDE back, Cait told Stuart what she'd learned from Bree about how the women of the village were setting up a new market. "They need a covered structure, so their goods are not exposed to the weather."

He nodded. "I will be sure to tell Dougal, though I am certain he will hear of it from his own wife."

"Cait?" Stuart reached for her hand. "Why do ye sleep with yer back to me?"

Her eyes widened not sure how to respond. She'd turned away so that he would not see the look of disappointment when he didn't attempt to make love to her. He did pull her close, but other than a quick kiss, he'd not done more.

"Ye are recovering I know ye need time to gain yer strength. I had to sleep with my back to ye while ye were… ill."

"Is there something ye are not telling me? Did seeing me without the ability to speak or see ye change yer feelings toward me?"

"No!" Cait threw her arms around him. "I love ye more each day."

Stuart's body slumped with relief and he pressed his mouth

to hers, kissing her with so much desperation, she could scarcely breathe.

"I want ye." The huskiness in his voice brought tingles of awareness and Cait pressed kisses to his neck, enjoying his sounds of encouragement.

He pushed away and peered out grunting with annoyance. "I never thought the ride home to be so long."

Upon arriving, they dashed past a startled Grace who announced last meal would be a bit late as they'd not expected them to return until the following day.

Later Cait would be mortified at the woman's chuckle. In that moment, however, all she wanted was to be alone with her husband.

Stuart had lost weight, but he was still magnificent when unclothed. When he stalked to the bed where she lay, Cait did not hide her appreciation of what she saw.

He climbed into bed and peered down at her. It was exciting and somewhat a bit disconcerting to be so exposed to him. However, when Stuart trailed his hands from her shoulders over her breasts and down her stomach, Cait lost all inhibitions and reached for him.

There wasn't any need for a longer preamble, Stuart drove into her and both moaned at the joining. When he began to thrust Cait urged him on, lifting her hips to meet each thrust.

Heat pooled at her very core and she didn't fight it. More than anything, she needed to feel that Stuart was alive and that he was hers.

She'd never felt more blissful than at that moment. And when she crested, it was impossible to keep from sobbing with joy.

Hands firmly on her hips, her husband plunged just once more before a low moan erupted and his entire body shuddered with his own release.

Cradled against him as they regained their breathing, Cait sniffed loudly. "It was so emotional. So very wonderful."

"I agree," Stuart said pressing kisses to her face. "Does this mean, ye will not turn away tonight?"

Cait nodded. "I will sleep with my face toward ye." She let out a long breath before continuing, "I have news."

Studying her, Stuart frowned. "Good or bad?"

"Good," Cait giggled nervously. "We are to become parents."

Her strong, brave husband paled. He stared at her with round eyes but didn't speak. For a moment she thought he'd faint.

"Stuart? Did ye hear me?"

It was then she noticed a tear sliding down his face. He nodded, still unable to speak. Instead, he pulled her against him and held her tightly.

Cait stroked his hair. "We will be very happy forever."

# EPILOGUE

*1603, Ross Keep, South Uist Hebrides, Scotland*

"INTERESTING THAT SUDDENLY all my brothers are settling down," Caelan told his stepmother, Lady Mariel. "I will not fall into such a trap."

His stepmother chuckled. "I assure ye it is not a trap. I hope that when ye finally fall in love, it will not feel like one."

They sat in the parlor at Keep Ross. He'd arrived that evening as she'd asked him to take her to visit his half brother Stuart and wife Cait who lived on the west side of the Isle in a place called Eilean Daes.

His eldest half brother, and laird, Darach would not leave the keep until his wife, Isobel, was fully recovered from childbirth.

The other half brothers also could not leave their duties. Ewan was busy preparing his lands for winter, Gideon had gone to the southern guard post and Duncan's wife, Beatrice, was about to give birth soon. That left him to help with what needed to be done when it came to his stepmother.

He didn't begrudge having to travel. In actuality, he looked forward to seeing his half brother and visiting the village now that it was fully rebuilt. Although, he'd never admit it to them, he missed Stuart and his cousin, Artair, who remained at Eilean Daes, and he looked forward to spending time with them.

"When do ye wish to leave?" Caelan asked, drinking the last of the tea in his cup. "Early in the morning?"

"That would be perfect," his stepmother replied, eyes bright with excitement. "Oh did I mention we have another person traveling with us?"

Caelan let out a breath. "No, ye had not. Who?"

Just then a young woman walked in. Her clear green gaze barely hesitated on him before she looked to his stepmother and smiled widely. "I am sorry, I did not know ye had company."

"Nonsense," Lady Mariel said motioning to Caelan. "This is my stepson, Caelan. He is to take us to visit Stuart and his wife, Cait."

"Oh." The woman looked back to him. "I do not believe we have met."

His stepmother placed a hand on his forearm. "I do not suppose ye have. When Glynis visited last, ye were gone to the lowlands."

At the words, the woman studied him. "Ah yes, now I remember, ye are the brother who is more English than Scot."

The words made Caelan want to glare at her. Instead, he gave her a bland smile. "Is it more Scottish than English to state things one knows nothing of upon meeting someone for the first time?"

Glynis' eyes widened and she glanced to his stepmother. "I do not know why I said that. Father always says I have the worst habit of blurting things without thought." She looked back to Caelan. "Please forgive me."

When she lowered her gaze, Caelan studied her. Whoever

she was she had to be the most enticing woman he'd ever laid eyes on. Her plump lips begging for a lingering kiss. Her round curves an invitation to pleasure. Her breasts—

"Caelan?" His mother gave him a curious look. "Accept Glynis's apology."

His lips curved. "Of course. It is forgotten"

Satisfied, his stepmother smiled. "Glynis is my niece and is visiting from Bara."

"Ah, a MacNeil," Caelan said as Glynis lowered to sit.

"Ye say it as if ye do not care for my clan," Glynis replied.

Caelan did not reply because if he were to be honest, there was but one MacNeil he definitely did not care for. A young man at his school in Glasgow that he'd never gotten along with. But it was not something that mattered any longer.

"We leave early in the morning." he stood and walked from the room, unwilling to look and see how the woman was probably assessing his choice of clothing.

He was well aware, he dressed much more English than Scottish.

I bet ye cannot wait to get yer hands on
Caelan and Glynis' story.

# A Note to Readers

Can't get enough of Beatrice and Duncan? Check out this extra epilogue. When Beatrice ignores Duncan's warnings and sneaks off to the village, things take a turn for the worse. If only she'd listened to her husband! Click Here!

# About the Author

*Enticing. Engaging. Romance.*

USA Today Bestselling Author Hildie McQueen writes strong brooding alphas who meet their match in feisty brave heroines. If you like stories with a mixture of passion, drama, and humor, you will love Hildie's storytelling where love wins every single time!

A fan of all things pink, Paris, and four-legged creatures, Hildie resides in eastern Georgia, USA, with her super-hero husband Kurt and three little yappy dogs.

Join my reader group on Facebook: bit.ly/31YCee1
Sign up for my newsletter and get a free book! goo.gl/jLzPTA
Visit her website at www.hildiemcqueen.com
Facebook: facebook.com/HildieMcQueen
Twitter: twitter.com/authorhildie
Instagram instagram.com/hildiemcqueenwriter

Made in the USA
Columbia, SC
19 September 2021

45756861R00162